HUMPHRIES · BOYLE · PEER · STRESING

VOLUME TWO

BOOM!
BOX

JONESY Volume Two, April 2017. Published by BOOM! Box, a division of Boom Entertainment, Inc., 5670 Wilshire Boulevard, Suite 450, Los Angeles, CA 90036-5679. Jonesy is ™ & © 2017 Sam Humphries and Caitlin Rose Boyle. Originally published in single magazine form as JONESY No. 5-8. ™ & © 2016 Sam Humphries and Caitlin Rose Boyle. All rights reserved. BOOM! Box™ and the BOOM! Box logo are trademarks of Boom Entertainment, Inc., registered in various countries and categories. All characters, events, and institutions depicted herein are fictional. Any similarity between any of the names, characters, persons, events, and/or institutions in this publication to actual names, characters, and persons, whether living or dead, events, and/or institutions is unintended and purely coincidental. BOOM! Box does not read or accept unsolicited submissions of ideas, stories, or artwork.

A catalog record of this book is available from OCLC and from the BOOM! Studios website, www.boom-studios.com, on the Librarians page. For more information regarding the CPSIA on this printed material, call: (203) 595-3636 and provide reference #RICH - 735422.

BOOM! Studios, 5670 Wilshire Boulevard, Suite 450, Los Angeles, CA 90036-5679. Printed in USA. First Printing.

ISBN: 978-1-60886-999-2, eISBN: 978-1-61398-670-7

DEDICATED TO

JEANINE

♥ ♥ ♥ SAM & CAITLIN

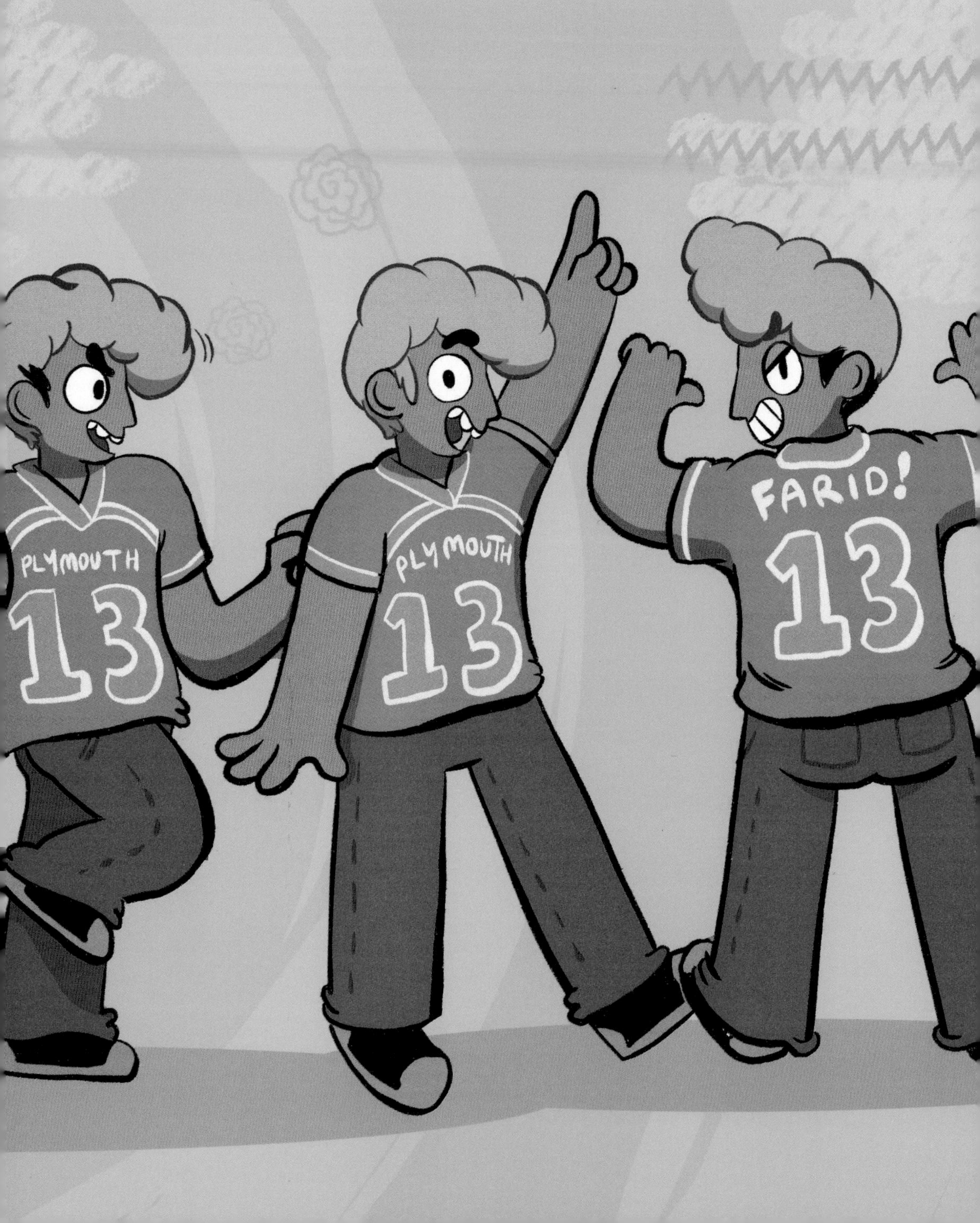
PLYMOUTH 13
PLYMOUTH 13
FARID! 13

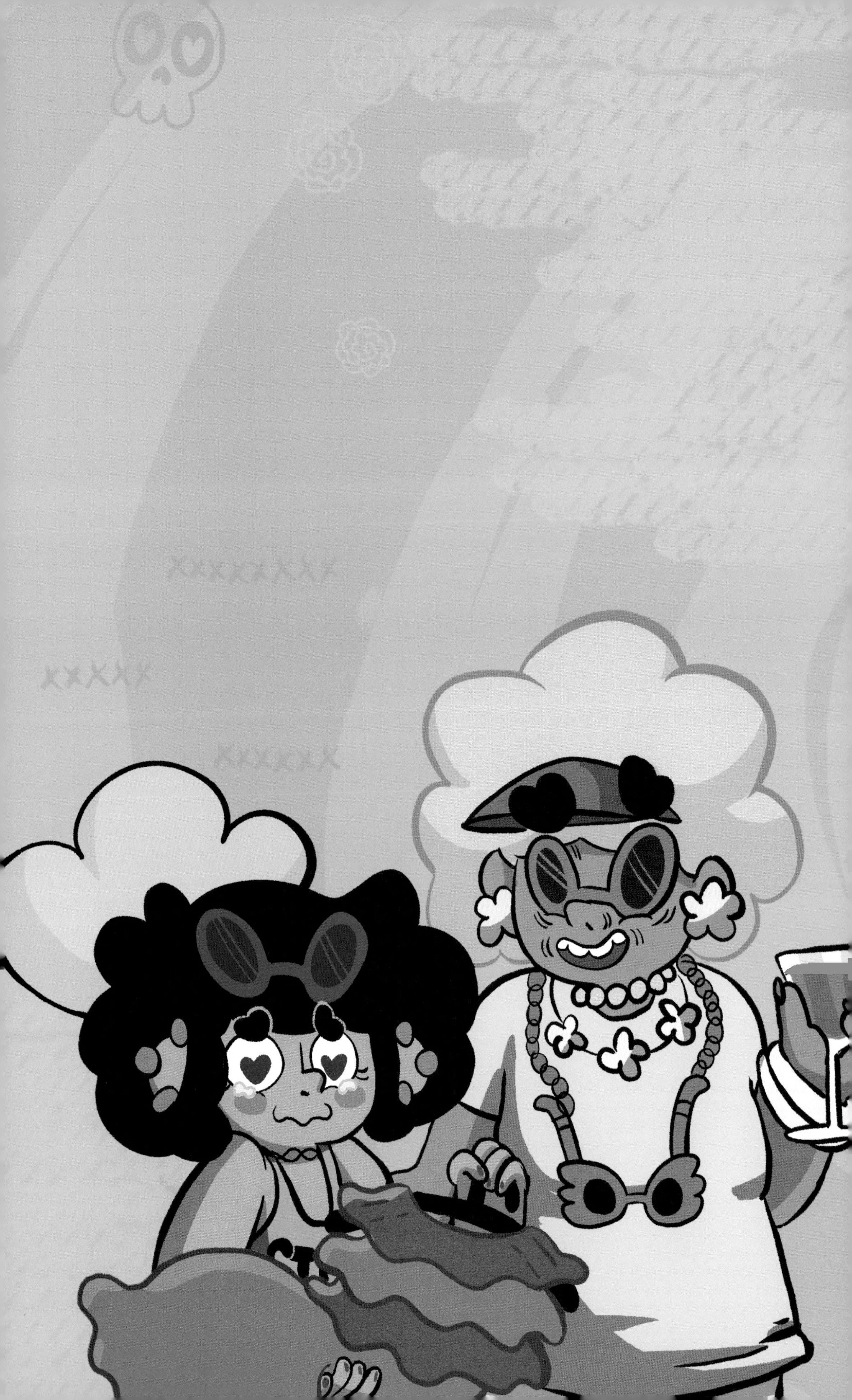

BY
SAM HUMPHRIES &
CAITLIN ROSE BOYLE

WITH COLORS BY
FRED C. STRESING CHAPTER 5
BRITTANY PEER CHAPTERS 6-8

LETTERS BY
COREY BREEN

COVER BY
CAITLIN ROSE BOYLE
WITH COLORS BY BRITTANY PEER

DESIGNER
KELSEY DIETERICH

ASSISTANT EDITOR
MATTHEW LEVINE

EDITORS
JEANINE SCHAEFER &
SHANNON WATTERS

CHAPTER ONE

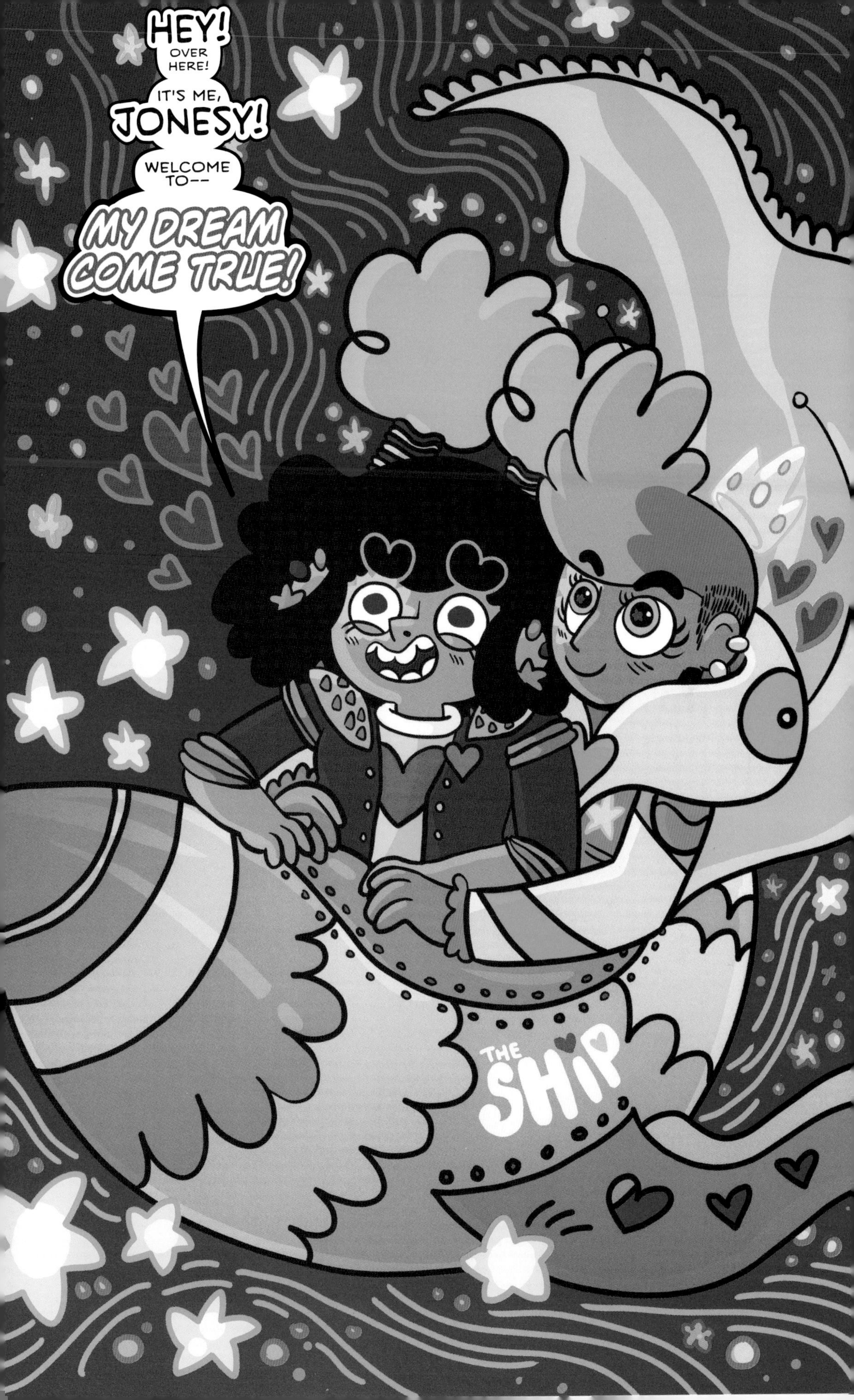
HEY! OVER HERE!
IT'S ME, JONESY!
WELCOME TO--
MY DREAM COME TRUE!
THE SHIP

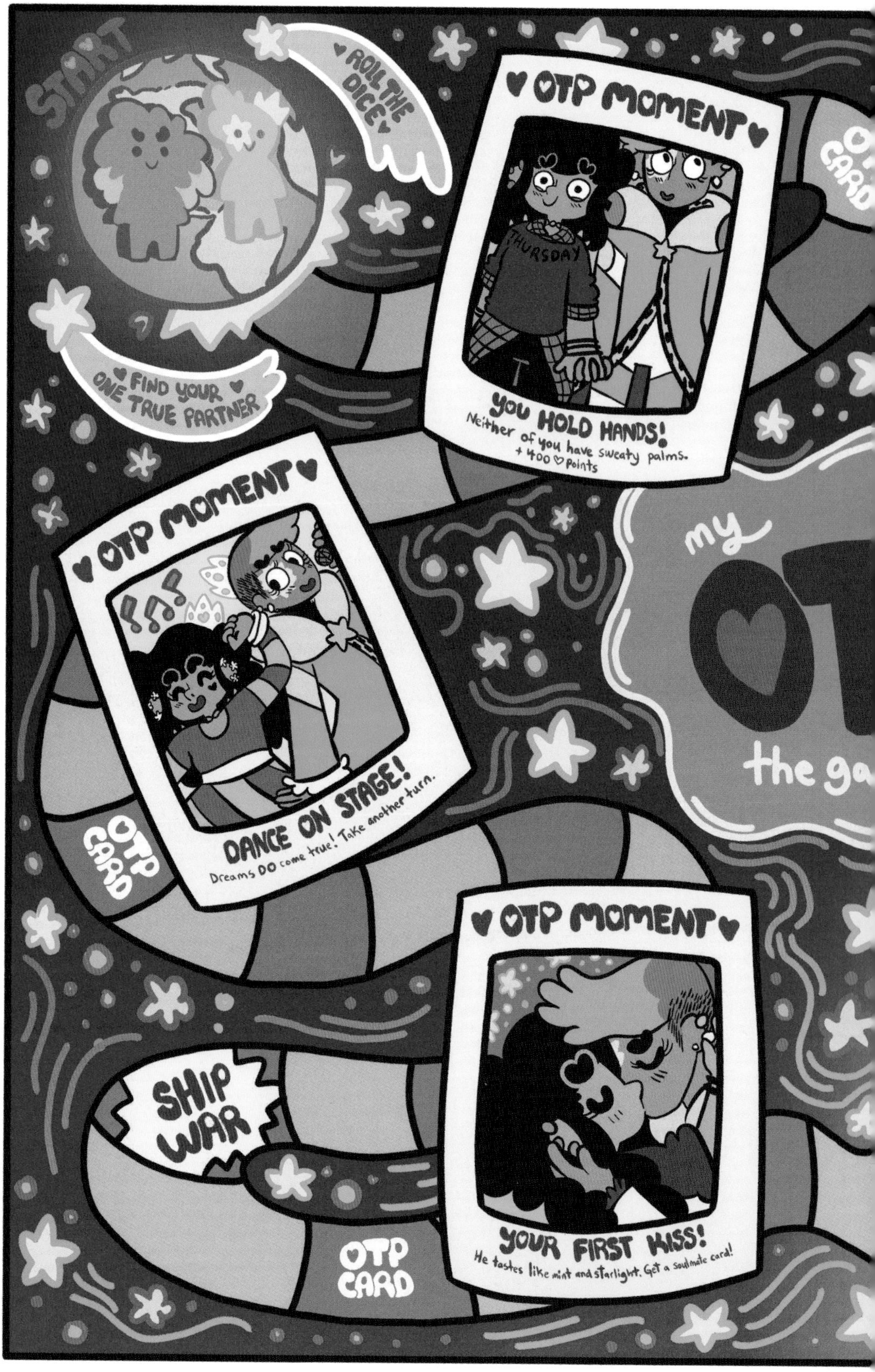
START
FIND YOUR ONE TRUE PARTNER
ROLL THE DICE
OTP MOMENT
THURSDAY
YOU HOLD HANDS!
Neither of you have sweaty palms.
+400 ♡ Points
OTP CARD
OTP MOMENT
DANCE ON STAGE!
Dreams DO come true! Take another turn.
OTP CARD
my OT
the ga
SHIP WAR
OTP MOMENT
YOUR FIRST KISS!
He tastes like mint and starlight. Get a soulmate card!
OTP CARD

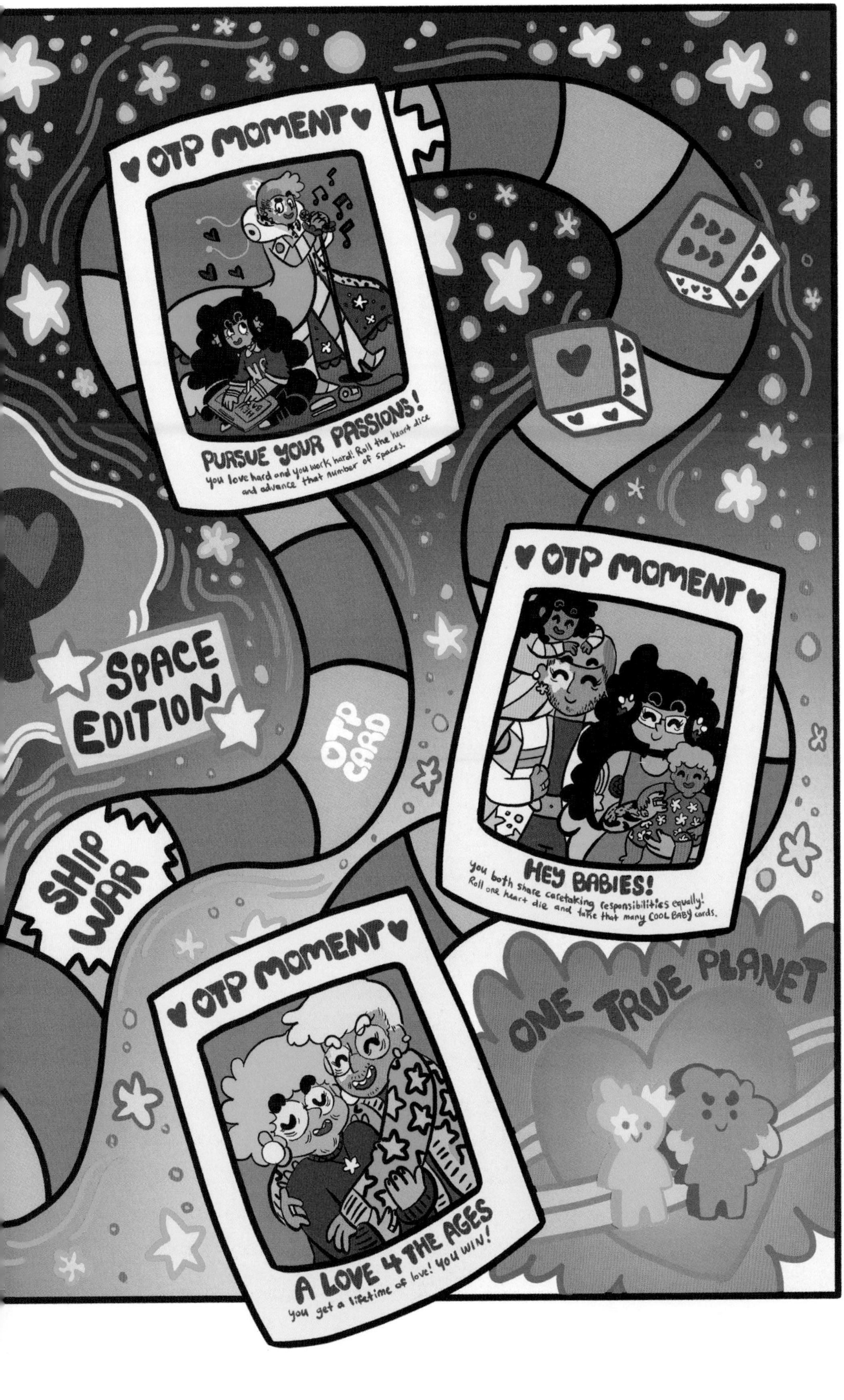
♥ OTP MOMENT ♥
PURSUE YOUR PASSIONS!
you love hard and you work hard! Roll the heart dice and advance that number of spaces.
SPACE EDITION
OTP CARD
SHIP WAR
♥ OTP MOMENT ♥
HEY BABIES!
you both share caretaking responsibilities equally! Roll one heart die and take that many COOL BABY cards.
♥ OTP MOMENT ♥
A LOVE 4 THE AGES
you get a lifetime of love! you WIN!
ONE TRUE PLANET

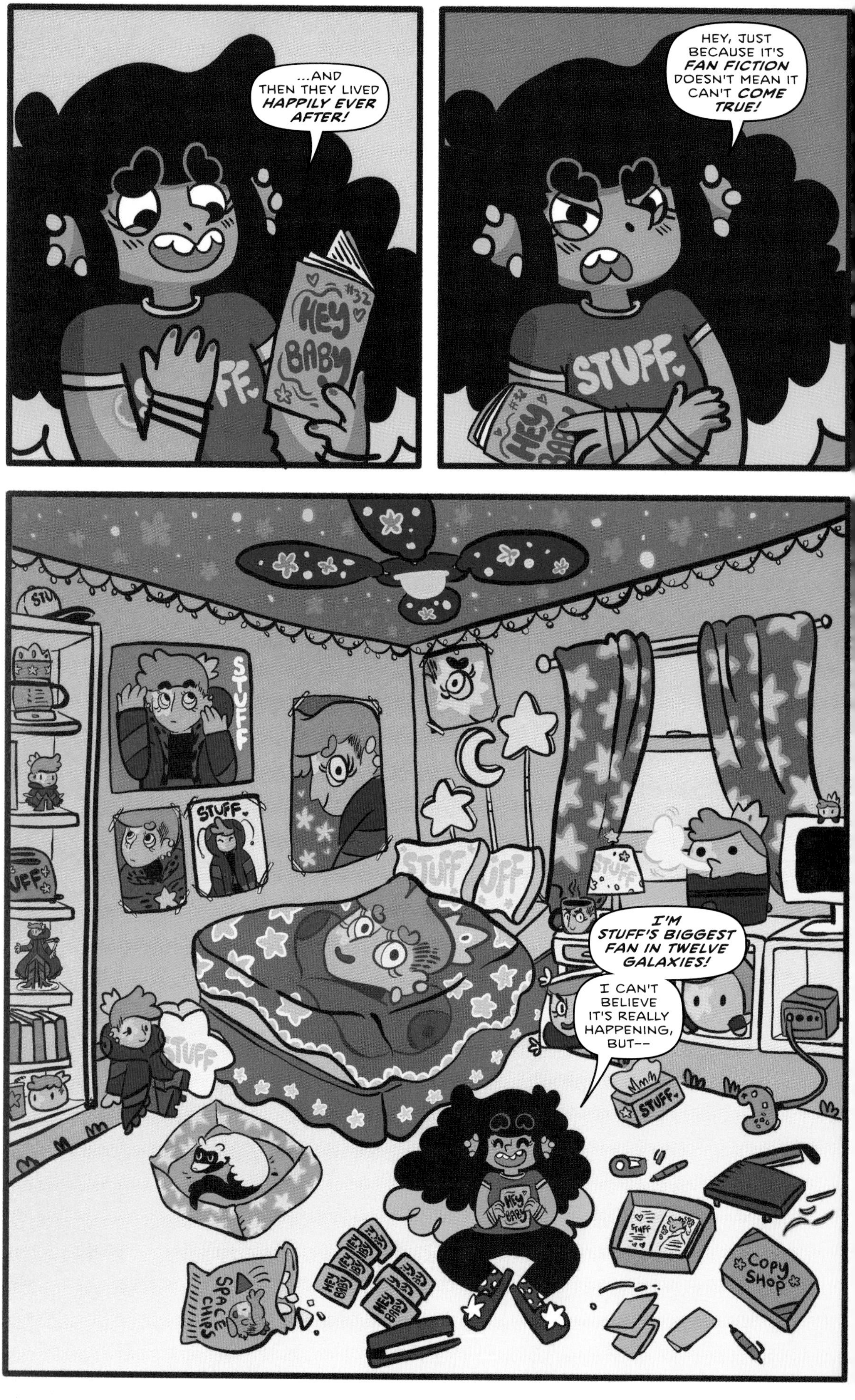

...AND THEN THEY LIVED HAPPILY EVER AFTER!
#32
HEY BABY
STUFF
HEY, JUST BECAUSE IT'S FAN FICTION DOESN'T MEAN IT CAN'T COME TRUE!
STUFF
I'M STUFF'S BIGGEST FAN IN TWELVE GALAXIES!
I CAN'T BELIEVE IT'S REALLY HAPPENING, BUT--
SPACE CHIPS
HEY BABY
Copy Shop

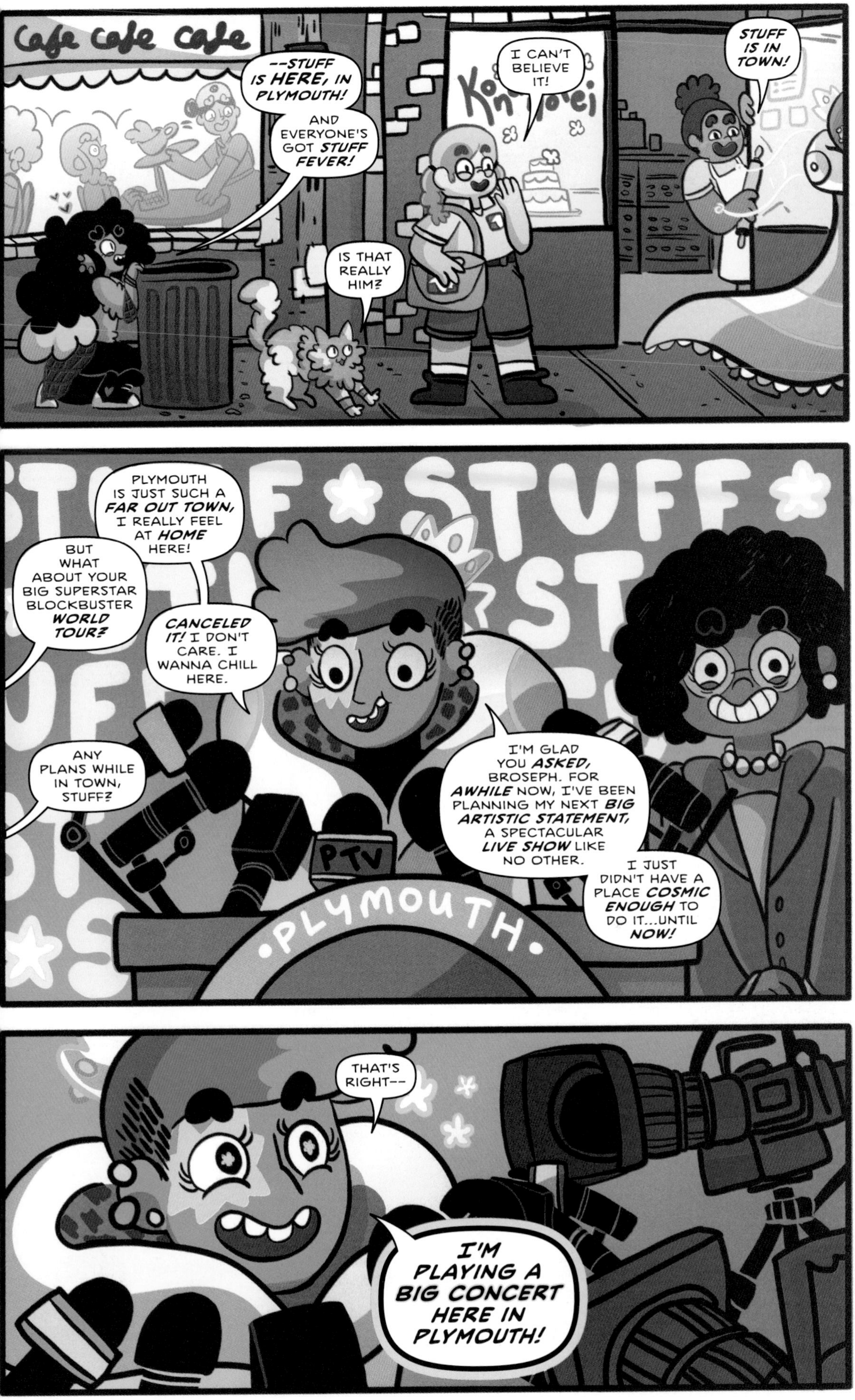
Cafe Cafe Cafe
--STUFF IS HERE, IN PLYMOUTH!
AND EVERYONE'S GOT STUFF FEVER!
I CAN'T BELIEVE IT!
STUFF IS IN TOWN!
IS THAT REALLY HIM?
STUFF
PLYMOUTH IS JUST SUCH A FAR OUT TOWN, I REALLY FEEL AT HOME HERE!
BUT WHAT ABOUT YOUR BIG SUPERSTAR BLOCKBUSTER WORLD TOUR?
CANCELED IT! I DON'T CARE. I WANNA CHILL HERE.
ANY PLANS WHILE IN TOWN, STUFF?
I'M GLAD YOU ASKED, BROSEPH. FOR AWHILE NOW, I'VE BEEN PLANNING MY NEXT BIG ARTISTIC STATEMENT, A SPECTACULAR LIVE SHOW LIKE NO OTHER.
I JUST DIDN'T HAVE A PLACE COSMIC ENOUGH TO DO IT...UNTIL NOW!
PTV
PLYMOUTH
THAT'S RIGHT--
I'M PLAYING A BIG CONCERT HERE IN PLYMOUTH!

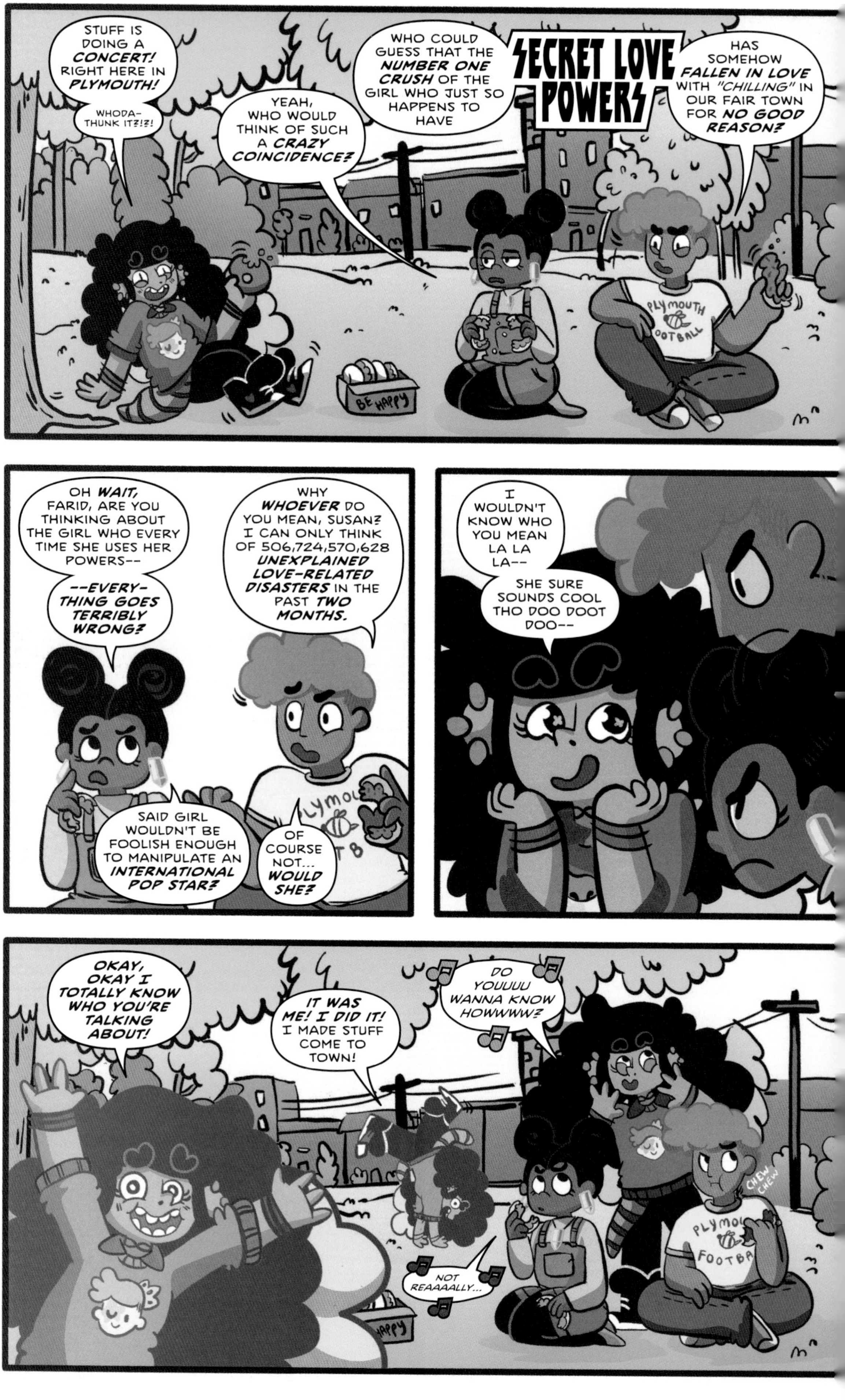

STUFF IS DOING A CONCERT! RIGHT HERE IN PLYMOUTH!
WHODA-THUNK IT?!?!
YEAH, WHO WOULD THINK OF SUCH A CRAZY COINCIDENCE?
WHO COULD GUESS THAT THE NUMBER ONE CRUSH OF THE GIRL WHO JUST SO HAPPENS TO HAVE
SECRET LOVE POWERS
HAS SOMEHOW FALLEN IN LOVE WITH "CHILLING" IN OUR FAIR TOWN FOR NO GOOD REASON?
BE HAPPY
PLYMOUTH FOOTBALL
OH WAIT, FARID, ARE YOU THINKING ABOUT THE GIRL WHO EVERY TIME SHE USES HER POWERS--
--EVERYTHING GOES TERRIBLY WRONG?
WHY WHOEVER DO YOU MEAN, SUSAN? I CAN ONLY THINK OF 506,724,570,628 UNEXPLAINED LOVE-RELATED DISASTERS IN THE PAST TWO MONTHS.
SAID GIRL WOULDN'T BE FOOLISH ENOUGH TO MANIPULATE AN INTERNATIONAL POP STAR?
OF COURSE NOT... WOULD SHE?
I WOULDN'T KNOW WHO YOU MEAN LA LA LA--
SHE SURE SOUNDS COOL THO DOO DOOT DOO--
OKAY, OKAY I TOTALLY KNOW WHO YOU'RE TALKING ABOUT!
IT WAS ME! I DID IT! I MADE STUFF COME TO TOWN!
DO YOUUUU WANNA KNOW HOWWWW?
NOT REAAAALLY...
CHEW CHEW

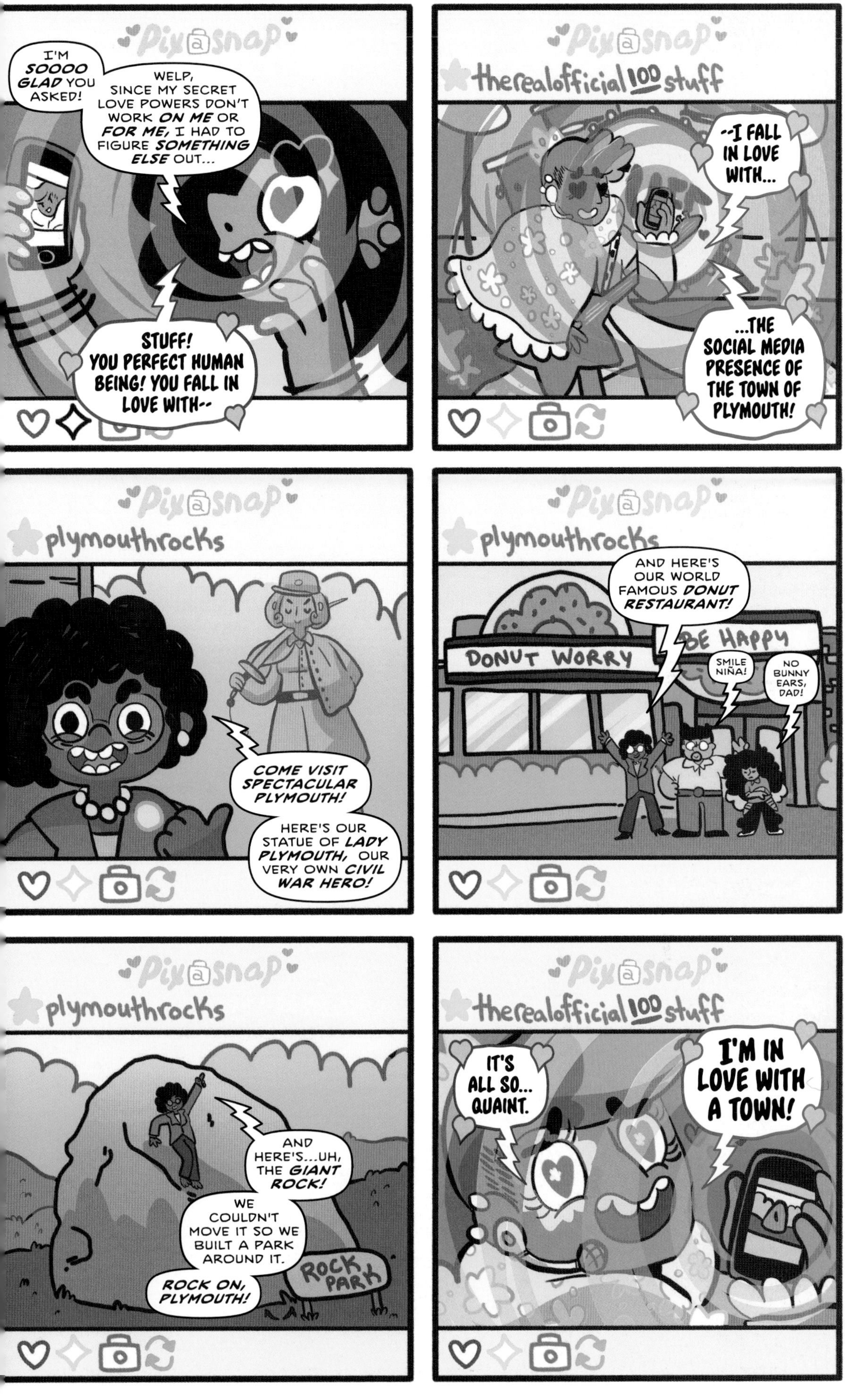
Pix@snap
I'M SOOOO GLAD YOU ASKED!
WELP, SINCE MY SECRET LOVE POWERS DON'T WORK ON ME OR FOR ME, I HAD TO FIGURE SOMETHING ELSE OUT...
STUFF! YOU PERFECT HUMAN BEING! YOU FALL IN LOVE WITH--
Pix@snap
therealofficial100stuff
--I FALL IN LOVE WITH...
...THE SOCIAL MEDIA PRESENCE OF THE TOWN OF PLYMOUTH!
Pix@snap
plymouthrocks
COME VISIT SPECTACULAR PLYMOUTH!
HERE'S OUR STATUE OF LADY PLYMOUTH, OUR VERY OWN CIVIL WAR HERO!
Pix@snap
plymouthrocks
AND HERE'S OUR WORLD FAMOUS DONUT RESTAURANT!
DONUT WORRY
BE HAPPY
SMILE NIÑA!
NO BUNNY EARS, DAD!
Pix@snap
plymouthrocks
AND HERE'S...UH, THE GIANT ROCK!
WE COULDN'T MOVE IT SO WE BUILT A PARK AROUND IT.
ROCK ON, PLYMOUTH!
ROCK PARK
Pix@snap
therealofficial100stuff
IT'S ALL SO... QUAINT.
I'M IN LOVE WITH A TOWN!

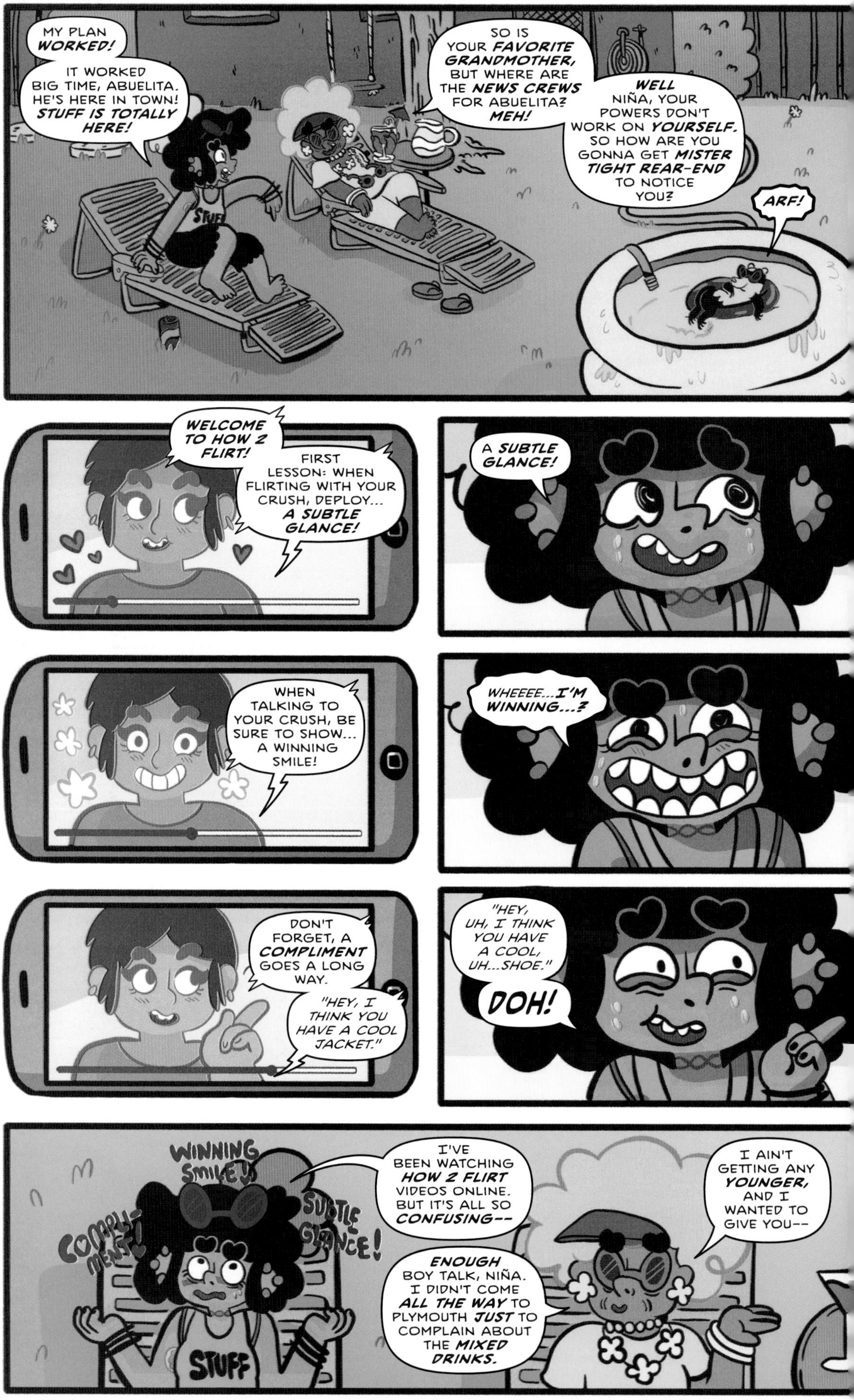
MY PLAN WORKED!
IT WORKED BIG TIME, ABUELITA. HE'S HERE IN TOWN! STUFF IS TOTALLY HERE!
SO IS YOUR FAVORITE GRANDMOTHER, BUT WHERE ARE THE NEWS CREWS FOR ABUELITA? MEH!
WELL NIÑA, YOUR POWERS DON'T WORK ON YOURSELF. SO HOW ARE YOU GONNA GET MISTER TIGHT REAR-END TO NOTICE YOU?
ARF!
STUFF
WELCOME TO HOW 2 FLIRT!
FIRST LESSON: WHEN FLIRTING WITH YOUR CRUSH, DEPLOY... A SUBTLE GLANCE!
A SUBTLE GLANCE!
WHEN TALKING TO YOUR CRUSH, BE SURE TO SHOW... A WINNING SMILE!
WHEEEE...I'M WINNING...?
DON'T FORGET, A COMPLIMENT GOES A LONG WAY.
"HEY, I THINK YOU HAVE A COOL JACKET."
"HEY, UH, I THINK YOU HAVE A COOL, UH...SHOE."
DOH!
WINNING SMILE
COMPLI-MENT!
SUBTLE GLANCE!
I'VE BEEN WATCHING HOW 2 FLIRT VIDEOS ONLINE. BUT IT'S ALL SO CONFUSING--
I AIN'T GETTING ANY YOUNGER, AND I WANTED TO GIVE YOU--
ENOUGH BOY TALK, NIÑA. I DIDN'T COME ALL THE WAY TO PLYMOUTH JUST TO COMPLAIN ABOUT THE MIXED DRINKS.
STUFF

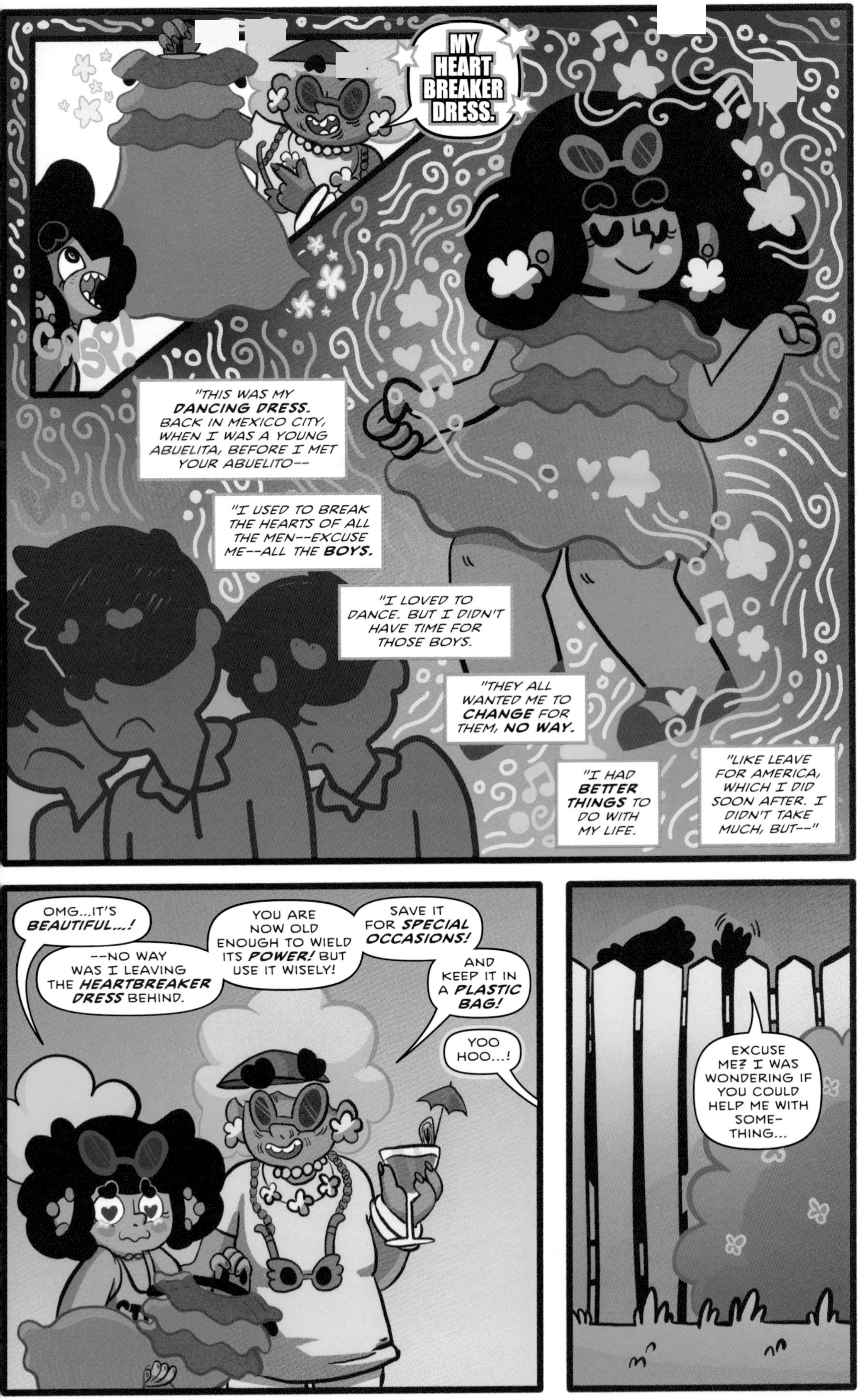
MY HEART BREAKER DRESS.
GASP!
"THIS WAS MY DANCING DRESS. BACK IN MEXICO CITY, WHEN I WAS A YOUNG ABUELITA, BEFORE I MET YOUR ABUELITO--
"I USED TO BREAK THE HEARTS OF ALL THE MEN--EXCUSE ME--ALL THE BOYS.
"I LOVED TO DANCE. BUT I DIDN'T HAVE TIME FOR THOSE BOYS.
"THEY ALL WANTED ME TO CHANGE FOR THEM, NO WAY.
"I HAD BETTER THINGS TO DO WITH MY LIFE.
"LIKE LEAVE FOR AMERICA, WHICH I DID SOON AFTER. I DIDN'T TAKE MUCH, BUT--"
OMG...IT'S BEAUTIFUL...!
--NO WAY WAS I LEAVING THE HEARTBREAKER DRESS BEHIND.
YOU ARE NOW OLD ENOUGH TO WIELD ITS POWER! BUT USE IT WISELY!
SAVE IT FOR SPECIAL OCCASIONS!
AND KEEP IT IN A PLASTIC BAG!
YOO HOO...!
EXCUSE ME? I WAS WONDERING IF YOU COULD HELP ME WITH SOME-THING...

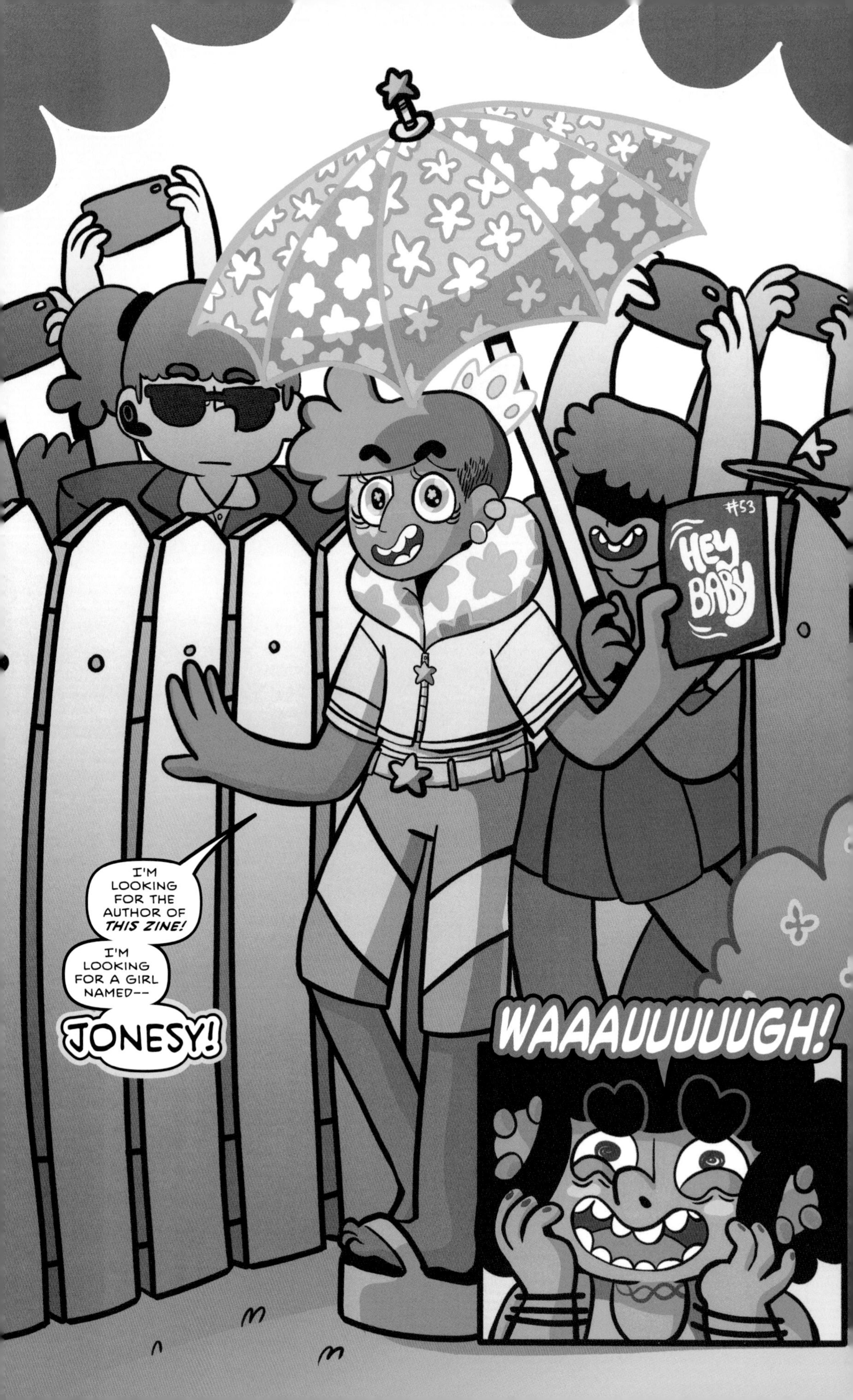
#53
HEY BABY
I'M LOOKING FOR THE AUTHOR OF THIS ZINE!
I'M LOOKING FOR A GIRL NAMED--
JONESY!
WAAAUUUUUGH!

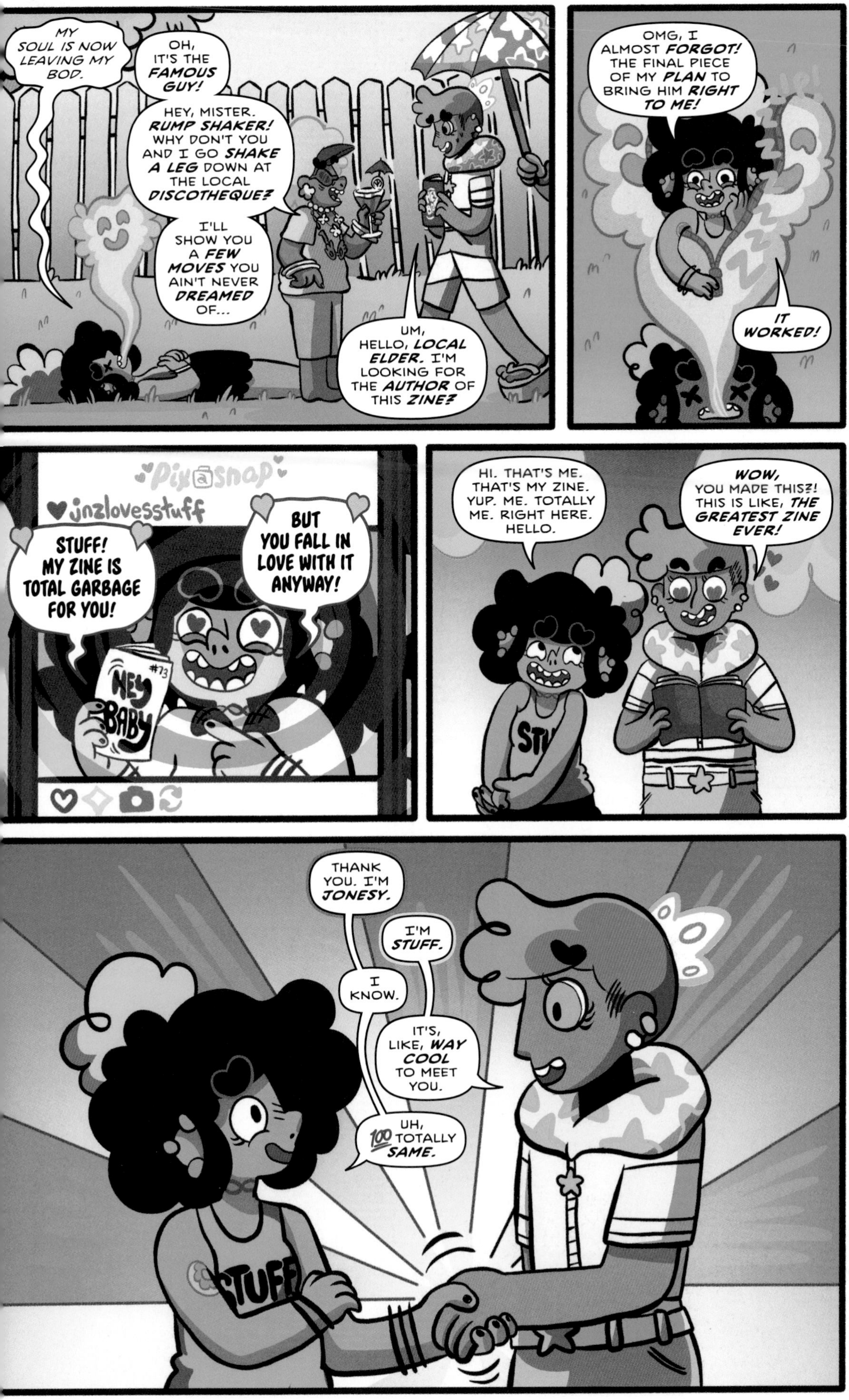
MY SOUL IS NOW LEAVING MY BOD.
OH, IT'S THE FAMOUS GUY!
HEY, MISTER. RUMP SHAKER! WHY DON'T YOU AND I GO SHAKE A LEG DOWN AT THE LOCAL DISCOTHEQUE?
I'LL SHOW YOU A FEW MOVES YOU AIN'T NEVER DREAMED OF...
UM, HELLO, LOCAL ELDER. I'M LOOKING FOR THE AUTHOR OF THIS ZINE?
OMG, I ALMOST FORGOT! THE FINAL PIECE OF MY PLAN TO BRING HIM RIGHT TO ME!
IT WORKED!
Pix@snap
♥jnzlovesstuff
STUFF! MY ZINE IS TOTAL GARBAGE FOR YOU!
BUT YOU FALL IN LOVE WITH IT ANYWAY!
#73
HEY BABY
HI. THAT'S ME. THAT'S MY ZINE. YUP. ME. TOTALLY ME. RIGHT HERE. HELLO.
WOW, YOU MADE THIS?! THIS IS LIKE, THE GREATEST ZINE EVER!
THANK YOU. I'M JONESY.
I'M STUFF.
I KNOW.
IT'S, LIKE, WAY COOL TO MEET YOU.
UH, 💯 TOTALLY SAME.
STUFF

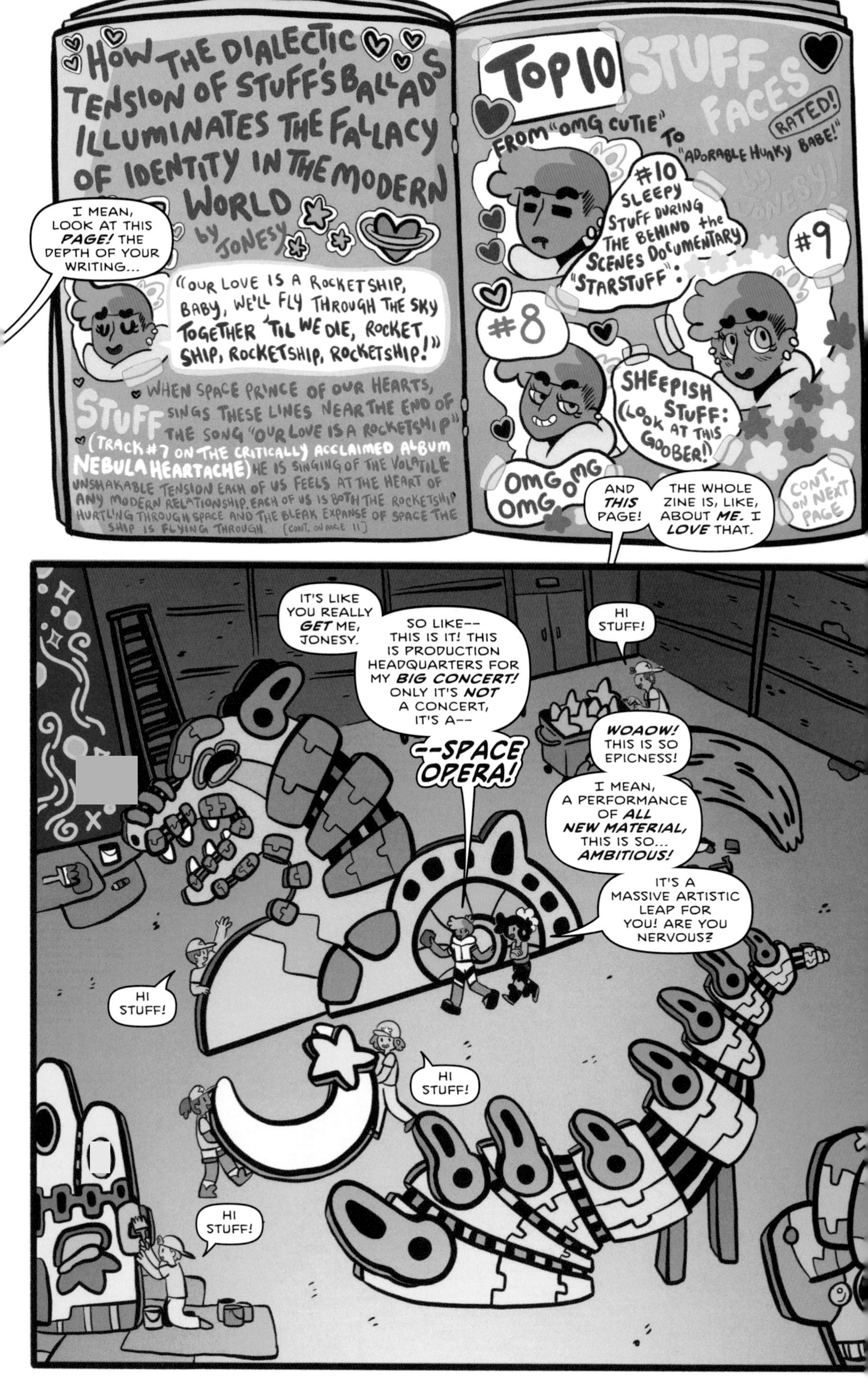
HOW THE DIALECTIC TENSION OF STUFF'S BALLADS ILLUMINATES THE FALLACY OF IDENTITY IN THE MODERN WORLD
by JONESY
"OUR LOVE IS A ROCKETSHIP, BABY, WE'LL FLY THROUGH THE SKY TOGETHER 'TIL WE DIE, ROCKET SHIP, ROCKETSHIP, ROCKETSHIP!"
WHEN SPACE PRINCE OF OUR HEARTS, STUFF SINGS THESE LINES NEAR THE END OF THE SONG "OUR LOVE IS A ROCKETSHIP" (TRACK #7 ON THE CRITICALLY ACCLAIMED ALBUM NEBULA HEARTACHE) HE IS SINGING OF THE VOLATILE UNSHAKABLE TENSION EACH OF US FEELS AT THE HEART OF ANY MODERN RELATIONSHIP. EACH OF US IS BOTH THE ROCKETSHIP HURTLING THROUGH SPACE AND THE BLEAK EXPANSE OF SPACE THE SHIP IS FLYING THROUGH. (CONT. ON PAGE 11)
I MEAN, LOOK AT THIS PAGE! THE DEPTH OF YOUR WRITING...
TOP 10 STUFF FACES RATED!
FROM "OMG CUTIE" TO "ADORABLE HUNKY BABE!"
by JONESY!
#10 SLEEPY STUFF DURING THE BEHIND the SCENES DOCUMENTARY "STARSTUFF":
#9
#8
SHEEPISH STUFF: (LOOK AT THIS GOOBER!)
OMG OMG OMG OMG
CONT. ON NEXT PAGE
AND THIS PAGE!
THE WHOLE ZINE IS, LIKE, ABOUT ME. I LOVE THAT.
IT'S LIKE YOU REALLY GET ME, JONESY.
SO LIKE-- THIS IS IT! THIS IS PRODUCTION HEADQUARTERS FOR MY BIG CONCERT! ONLY IT'S NOT A CONCERT, IT'S A--
--SPACE OPERA!
HI STUFF!
WOAOW! THIS IS SO EPICNESS!
I MEAN, A PERFORMANCE OF ALL NEW MATERIAL, THIS IS SO... AMBITIOUS!
IT'S A MASSIVE ARTISTIC LEAP FOR YOU! ARE YOU NERVOUS?
HI STUFF!
HI STUFF!
HI STUFF!

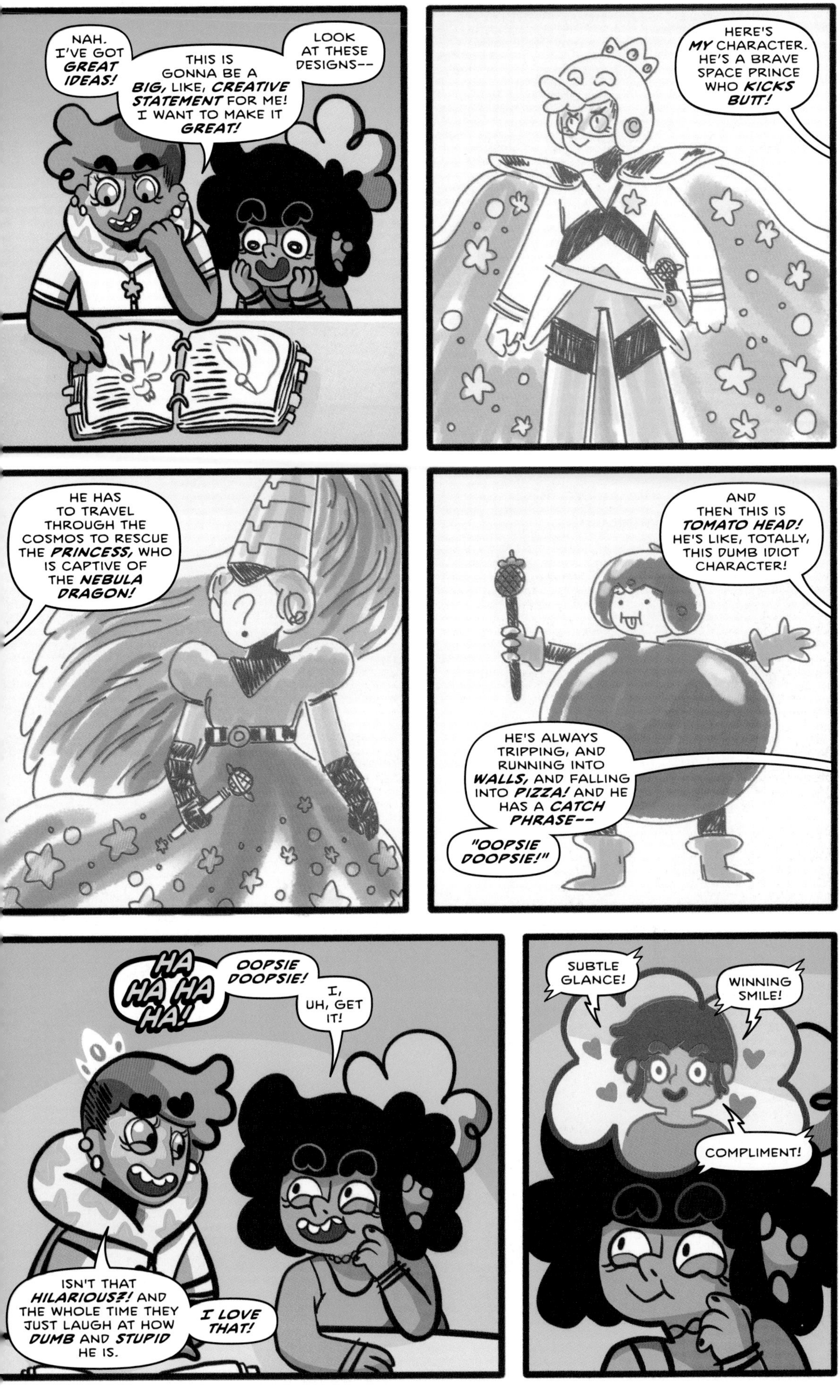
NAH. I'VE GOT GREAT IDEAS!
THIS IS GONNA BE A BIG, LIKE, CREATIVE STATEMENT FOR ME! I WANT TO MAKE IT GREAT!
LOOK AT THESE DESIGNS--
HERE'S MY CHARACTER. HE'S A BRAVE SPACE PRINCE WHO KICKS BUTT!
HE HAS TO TRAVEL THROUGH THE COSMOS TO RESCUE THE PRINCESS, WHO IS CAPTIVE OF THE NEBULA DRAGON!
AND THEN THIS IS TOMATO HEAD! HE'S LIKE, TOTALLY, THIS DUMB IDIOT CHARACTER!
HE'S ALWAYS TRIPPING, AND RUNNING INTO WALLS, AND FALLING INTO PIZZA! AND HE HAS A CATCH PHRASE--
"OOPSIE DOOPSIE!"
HA HA HA HA!
OOPSIE DOOPSIE!
I, UH, GET IT!
ISN'T THAT HILARIOUS?! AND THE WHOLE TIME THEY JUST LAUGH AT HOW DUMB AND STUPID HE IS.
I LOVE THAT!
SUBTLE GLANCE!
WINNING SMILE!
COMPLIMENT!

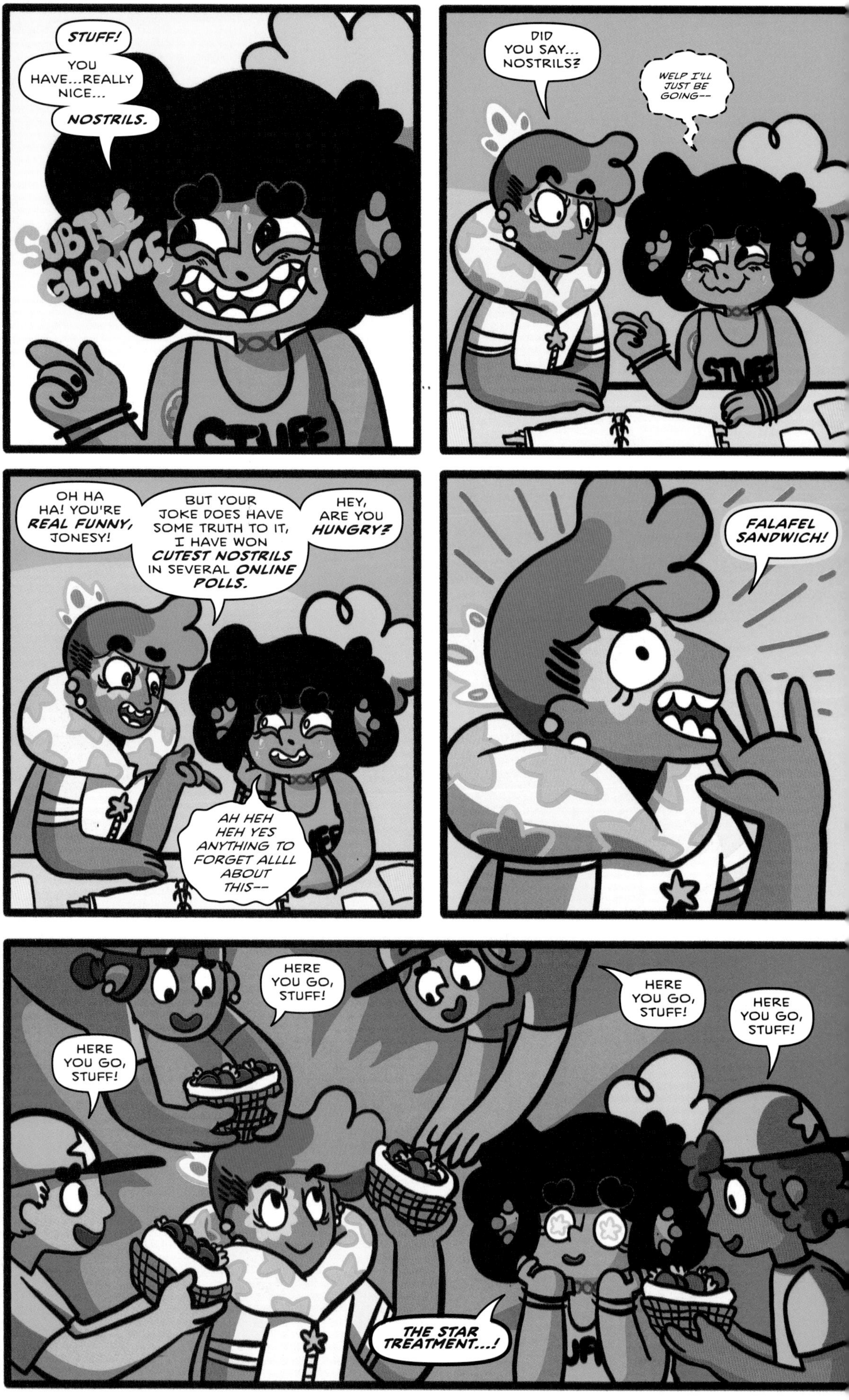
STUFF!
YOU HAVE...REALLY NICE...
NOSTRILS.
SUBTLE GLANCE
DID YOU SAY... NOSTRILS?
WELP I'LL JUST BE GOING--
STUFF
OH HA HA! YOU'RE REAL FUNNY, JONESY!
BUT YOUR JOKE DOES HAVE SOME TRUTH TO IT, I HAVE WON CUTEST NOSTRILS IN SEVERAL ONLINE POLLS.
HEY, ARE YOU HUNGRY?
AH HEH HEH YES ANYTHING TO FORGET ALLLL ABOUT THIS--
FALAFEL SANDWICH!
HERE YOU GO, STUFF!
HERE YOU GO, STUFF!
HERE YOU GO, STUFF!
HERE YOU GO, STUFF!
THE STAR TREATMENT...!

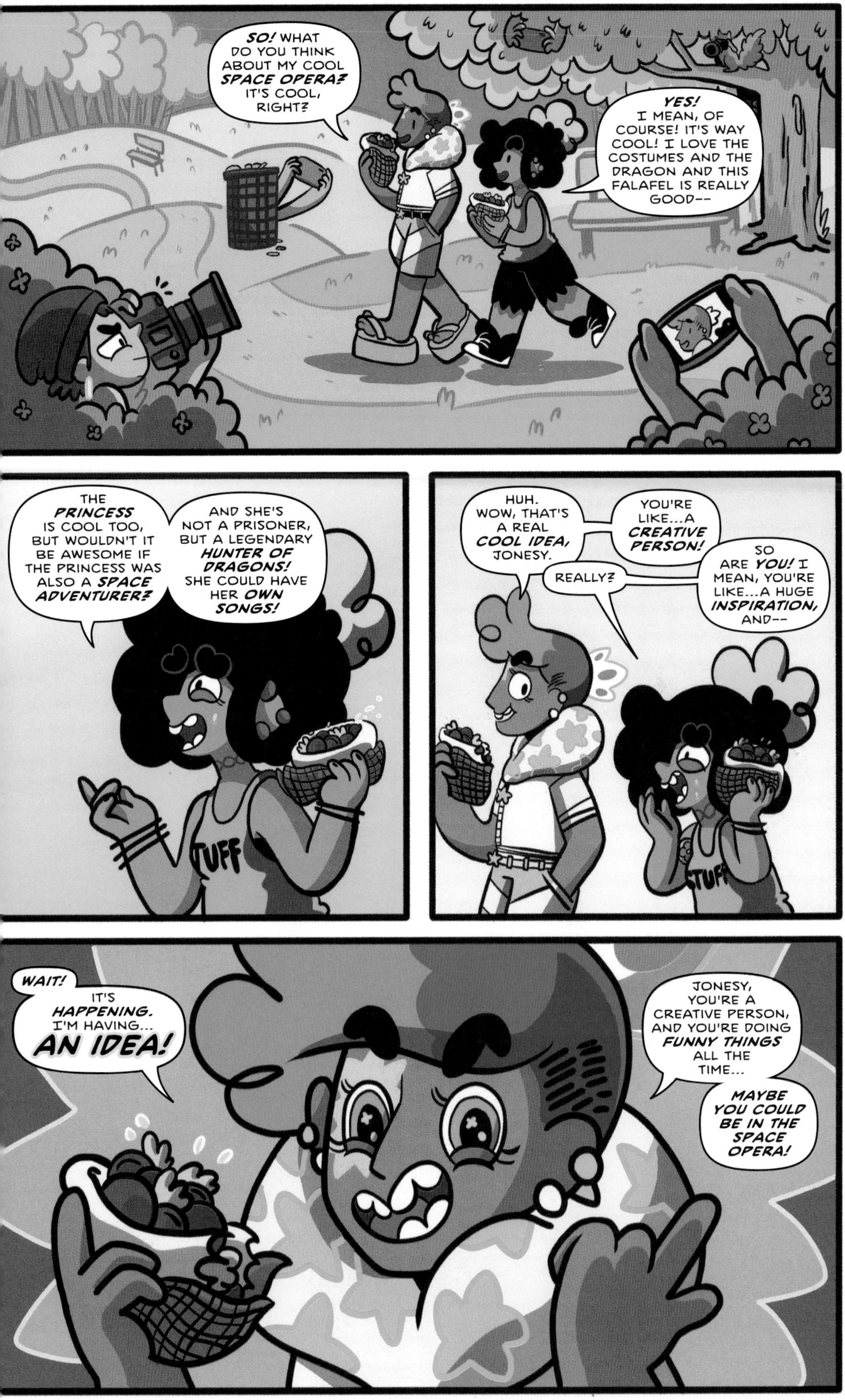
SO! WHAT DO YOU THINK ABOUT MY COOL SPACE OPERA? IT'S COOL, RIGHT?
YES! I MEAN, OF COURSE! IT'S WAY COOL! I LOVE THE COSTUMES AND THE DRAGON AND THIS FALAFEL IS REALLY GOOD--
THE PRINCESS IS COOL TOO, BUT WOULDN'T IT BE AWESOME IF THE PRINCESS WAS ALSO A SPACE ADVENTURER?
AND SHE'S NOT A PRISONER, BUT A LEGENDARY HUNTER OF DRAGONS! SHE COULD HAVE HER OWN SONGS!
TUFF
HUH. WOW, THAT'S A REAL COOL IDEA, JONESY.
YOU'RE LIKE...A CREATIVE PERSON!
REALLY?
SO ARE YOU! I MEAN, YOU'RE LIKE...A HUGE INSPIRATION, AND--
STUFF
WAIT! IT'S HAPPENING. I'M HAVING... AN IDEA!
JONESY, YOU'RE A CREATIVE PERSON, AND YOU'RE DOING FUNNY THINGS ALL THE TIME...
MAYBE YOU COULD BE IN THE SPACE OPERA!

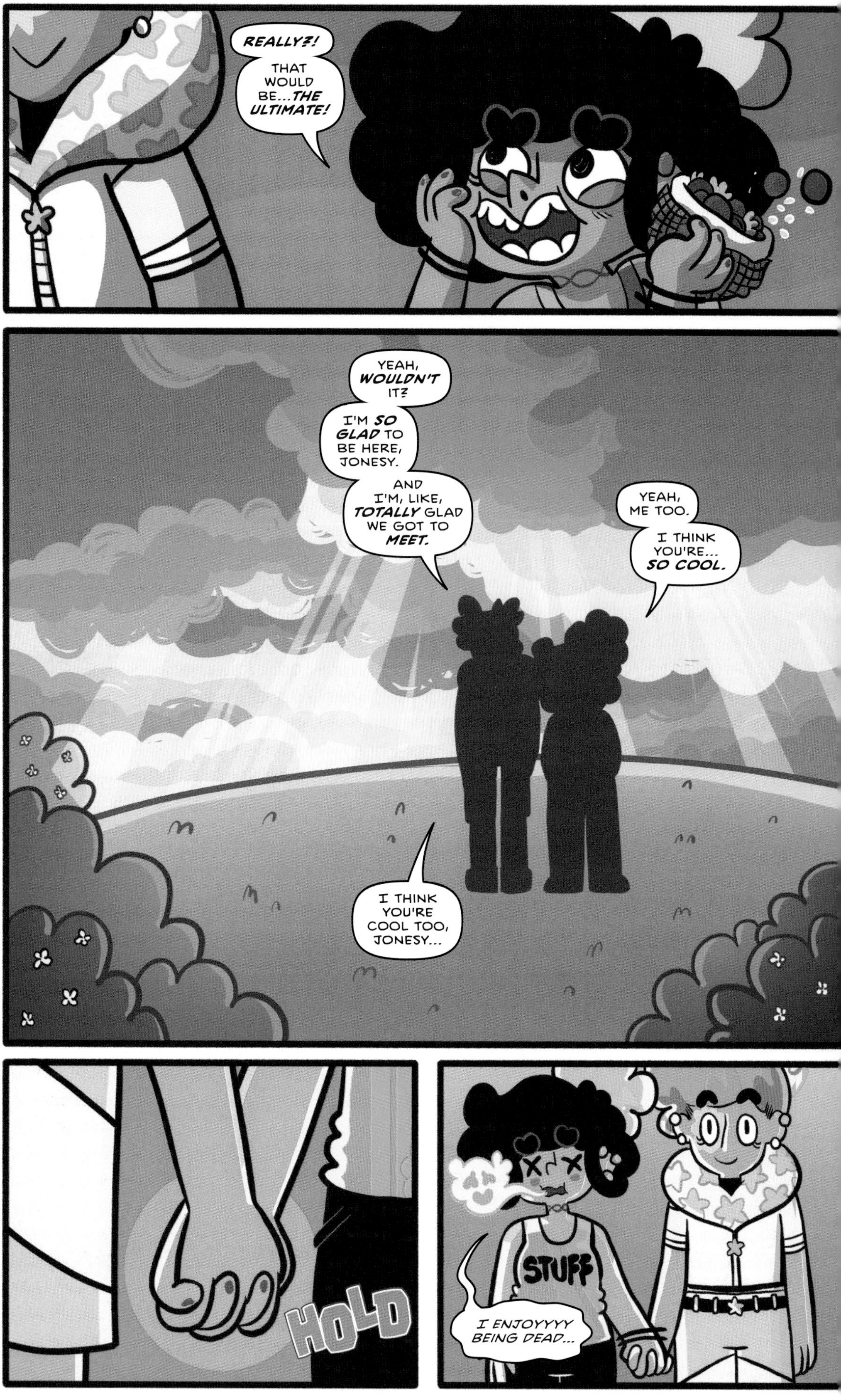
REALLY?! THAT WOULD BE...THE ULTIMATE!
YEAH, WOULDN'T IT?
I'M SO GLAD TO BE HERE, JONESY.
AND I'M, LIKE, TOTALLY GLAD WE GOT TO MEET.
YEAH, ME TOO.
I THINK YOU'RE... SO COOL.
I THINK YOU'RE COOL TOO, JONESY...
HOLD
STUFF
I ENJOYYYY BEING DEAD...

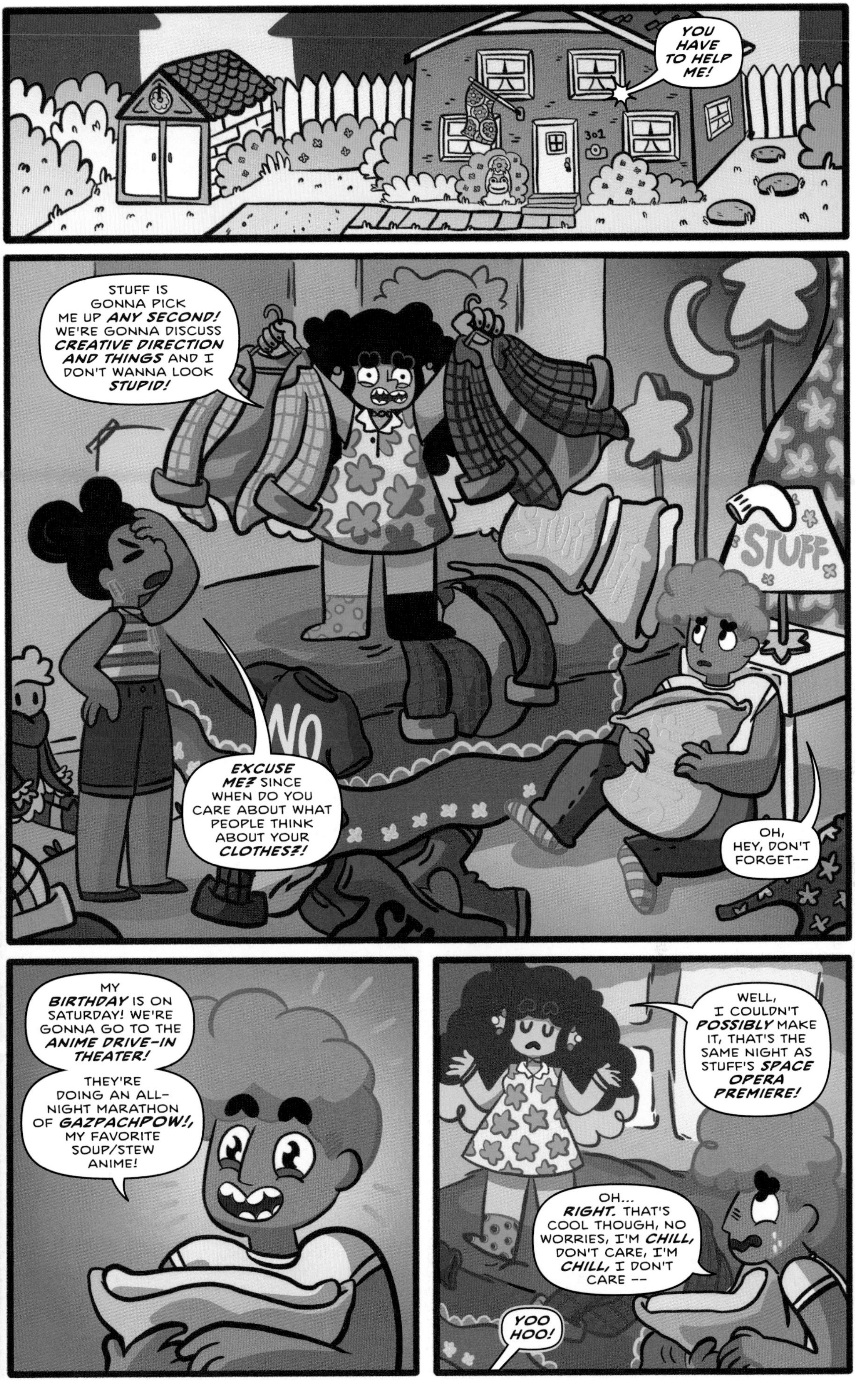
YOU HAVE TO HELP ME!
301
STUFF IS GONNA PICK ME UP ANY SECOND! WE'RE GONNA DISCUSS CREATIVE DIRECTION AND THINGS AND I DON'T WANNA LOOK STUPID!
STUFF
STUFF
NO
EXCUSE ME? SINCE WHEN DO YOU CARE ABOUT WHAT PEOPLE THINK ABOUT YOUR CLOTHES?!
OH, HEY, DON'T FORGET--
MY BIRTHDAY IS ON SATURDAY! WE'RE GONNA GO TO THE ANIME DRIVE-IN THEATER!
THEY'RE DOING AN ALL-NIGHT MARATHON OF GAZPACHPOW!, MY FAVORITE SOUP/STEW ANIME!
WELL, I COULDN'T POSSIBLY MAKE IT, THAT'S THE SAME NIGHT AS STUFF'S SPACE OPERA PREMIERE!
OH... RIGHT. THAT'S COOL THOUGH, NO WORRIES, I'M CHILL, DON'T CARE, I'M CHILL, I DON'T CARE --
YOO HOO!

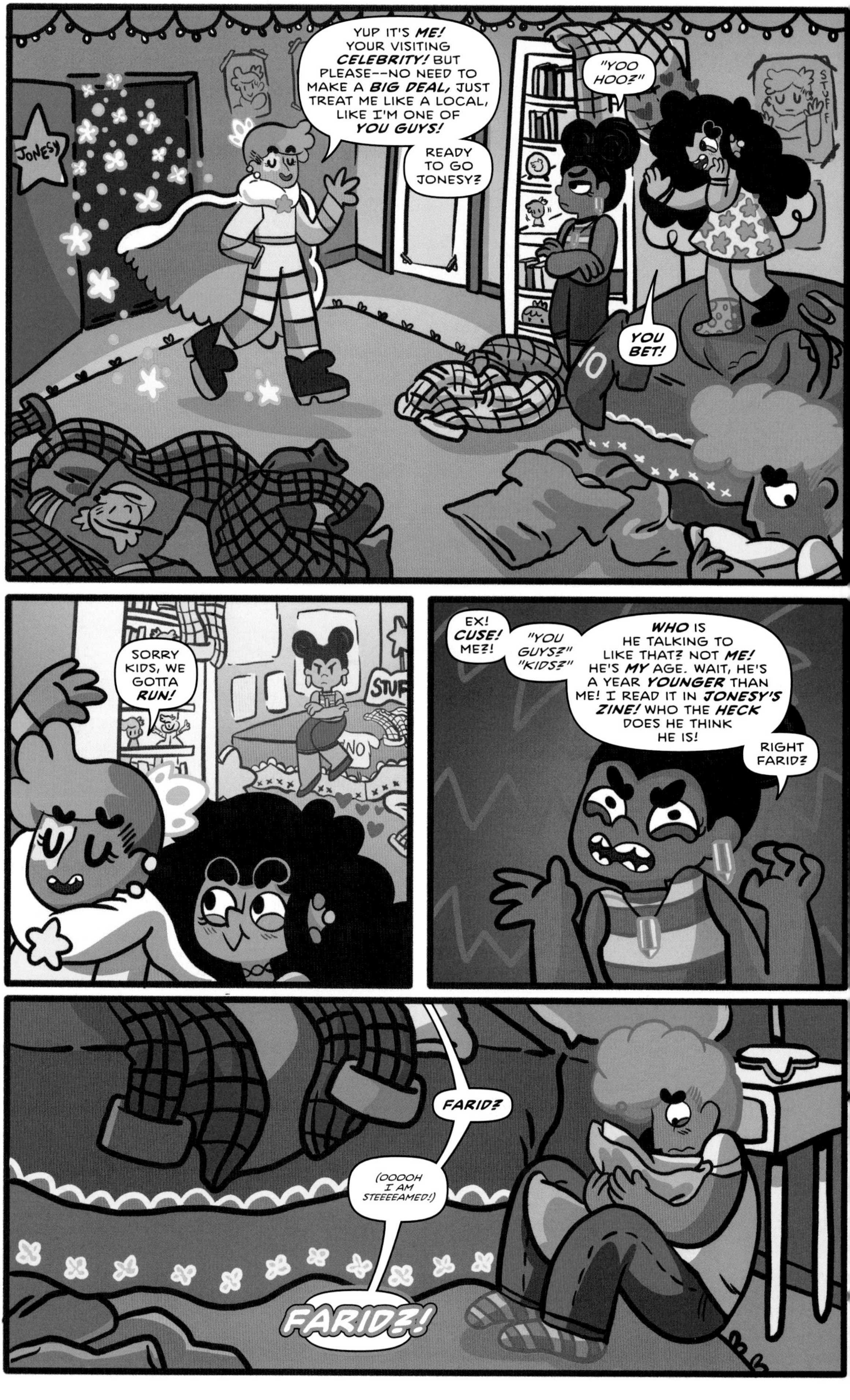
JONESY
YUP IT'S ME! YOUR VISITING CELEBRITY! BUT PLEASE--NO NEED TO MAKE A BIG DEAL, JUST TREAT ME LIKE A LOCAL, LIKE I'M ONE OF YOU GUYS!
READY TO GO JONESY?
"YOO HOO?"
STUFF
YOU BET!
NO
SORRY KIDS, WE GOTTA RUN!
STUF
EX! CUSE! ME?!
"YOU GUYS?" "KIDS?"
WHO IS HE TALKING TO LIKE THAT? NOT ME! HE'S MY AGE. WAIT, HE'S A YEAR YOUNGER THAN ME! I READ IT IN JONESY'S ZINE! WHO THE HECK DOES HE THINK HE IS!
RIGHT FARID?
FARID?
(OOOOH I AM STEEEEAMED!)
FARID?!

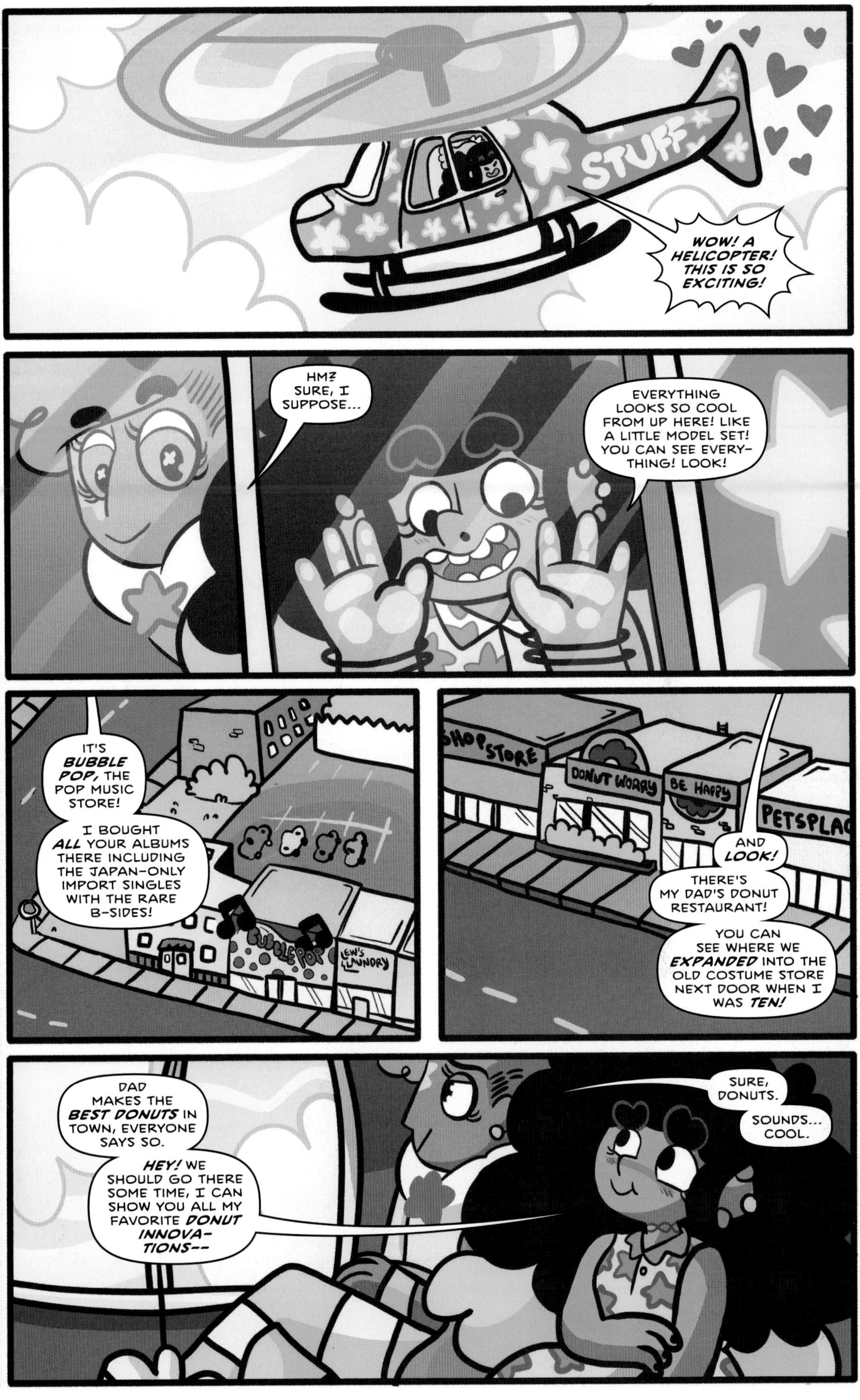
STUFF
WOW! A HELICOPTER! THIS IS SO EXCITING!
HM? SURE, I SUPPOSE...
EVERYTHING LOOKS SO COOL FROM UP HERE! LIKE A LITTLE MODEL SET! YOU CAN SEE EVERY-THING! LOOK!
IT'S BUBBLE POP, THE POP MUSIC STORE!
I BOUGHT ALL YOUR ALBUMS THERE INCLUDING THE JAPAN-ONLY IMPORT SINGLES WITH THE RARE B-SIDES!
BUBBLE POP
LEW'S LAUNDRY
SHOP STORE
DONUT WORRY
BE HAPPY
PETSPLAC
AND LOOK!
THERE'S MY DAD'S DONUT RESTAURANT!
YOU CAN SEE WHERE WE EXPANDED INTO THE OLD COSTUME STORE NEXT DOOR WHEN I WAS TEN!
DAD MAKES THE BEST DONUTS IN TOWN, EVERYONE SAYS SO.
HEY! WE SHOULD GO THERE SOME TIME, I CAN SHOW YOU ALL MY FAVORITE DONUT INNOVA-TIONS--
SURE, DONUTS.
SOUNDS... COOL.

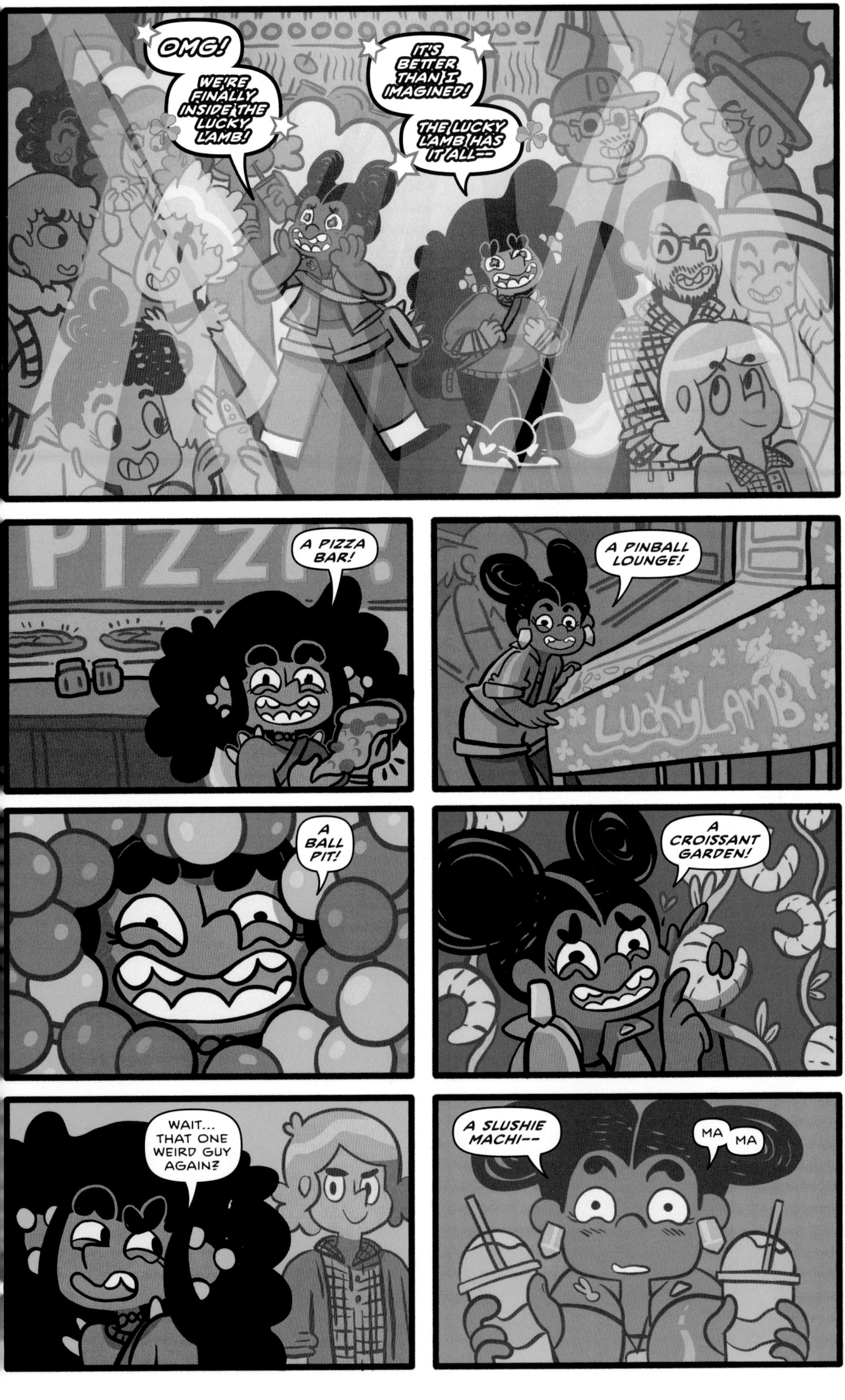
OMG!
WE'RE FINALLY INSIDE THE LUCKY LAMB!
IT'S BETTER THAN I IMAGINED!
THE LUCKY LAMB HAS IT ALL--
A PIZZA BAR!
A PINBALL LOUNGE!
LUCKY LAMB
A BALL PIT!
A CROISSANT GARDEN!
WAIT... THAT ONE WEIRD GUY AGAIN?
A SLUSHIE MACHI--
MA
MA

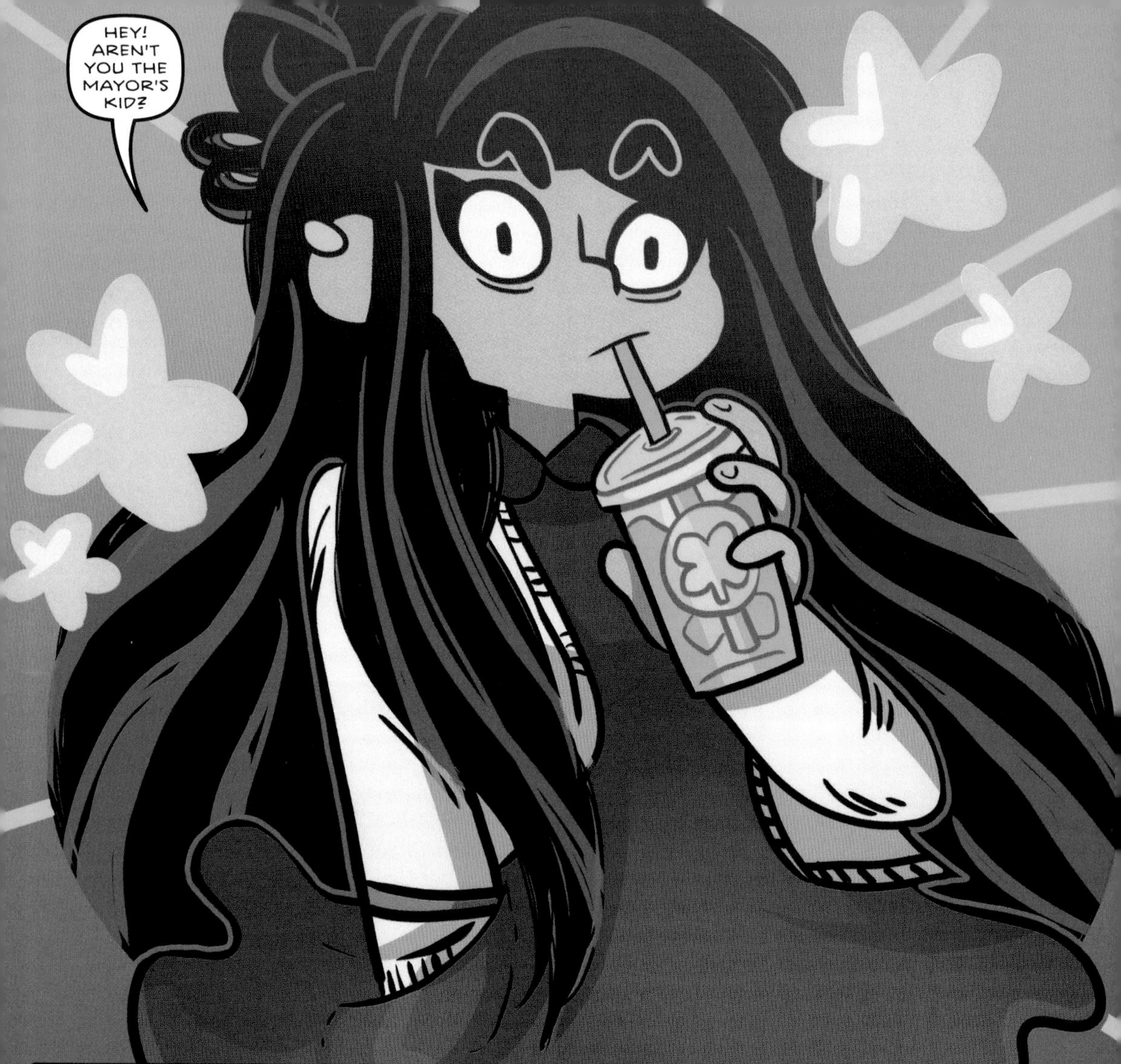
HEY!
AREN'T
YOU THE
MAYOR'S
KID?

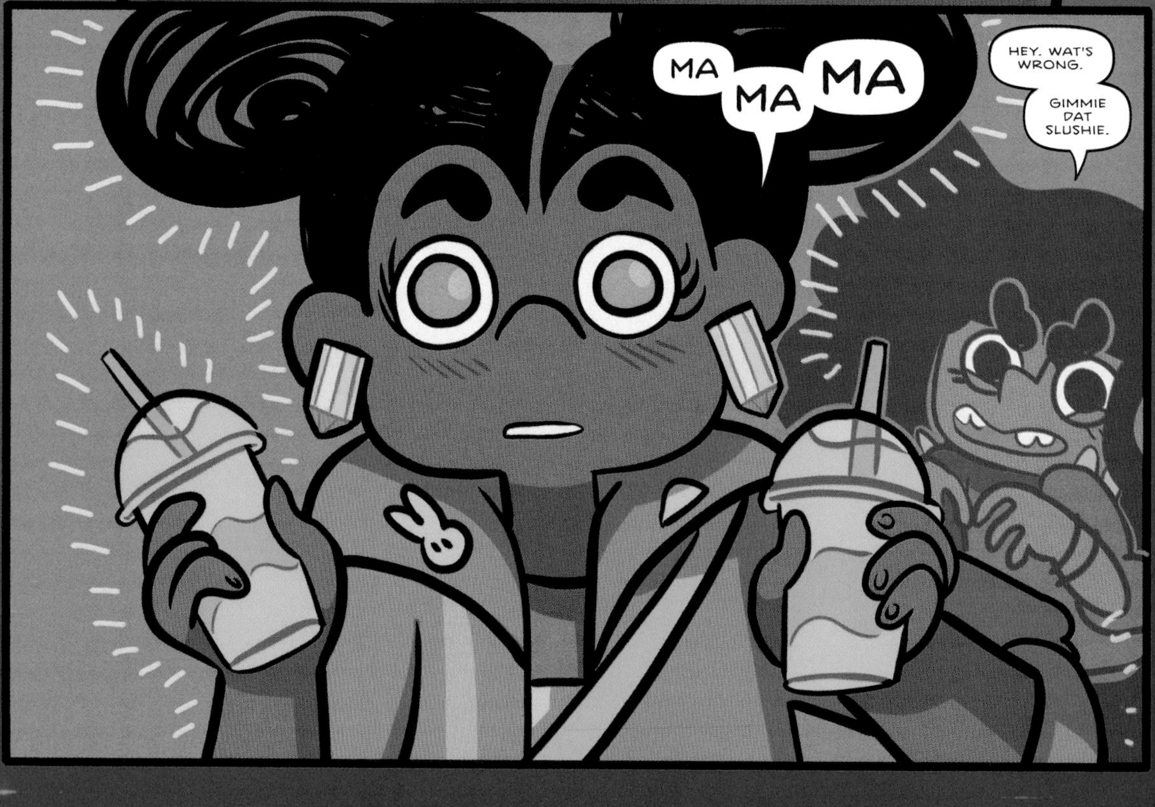
MA
MA
MA
HEY. WAT'S
WRONG.
GIMMIE
DAT
SLUSHIE.

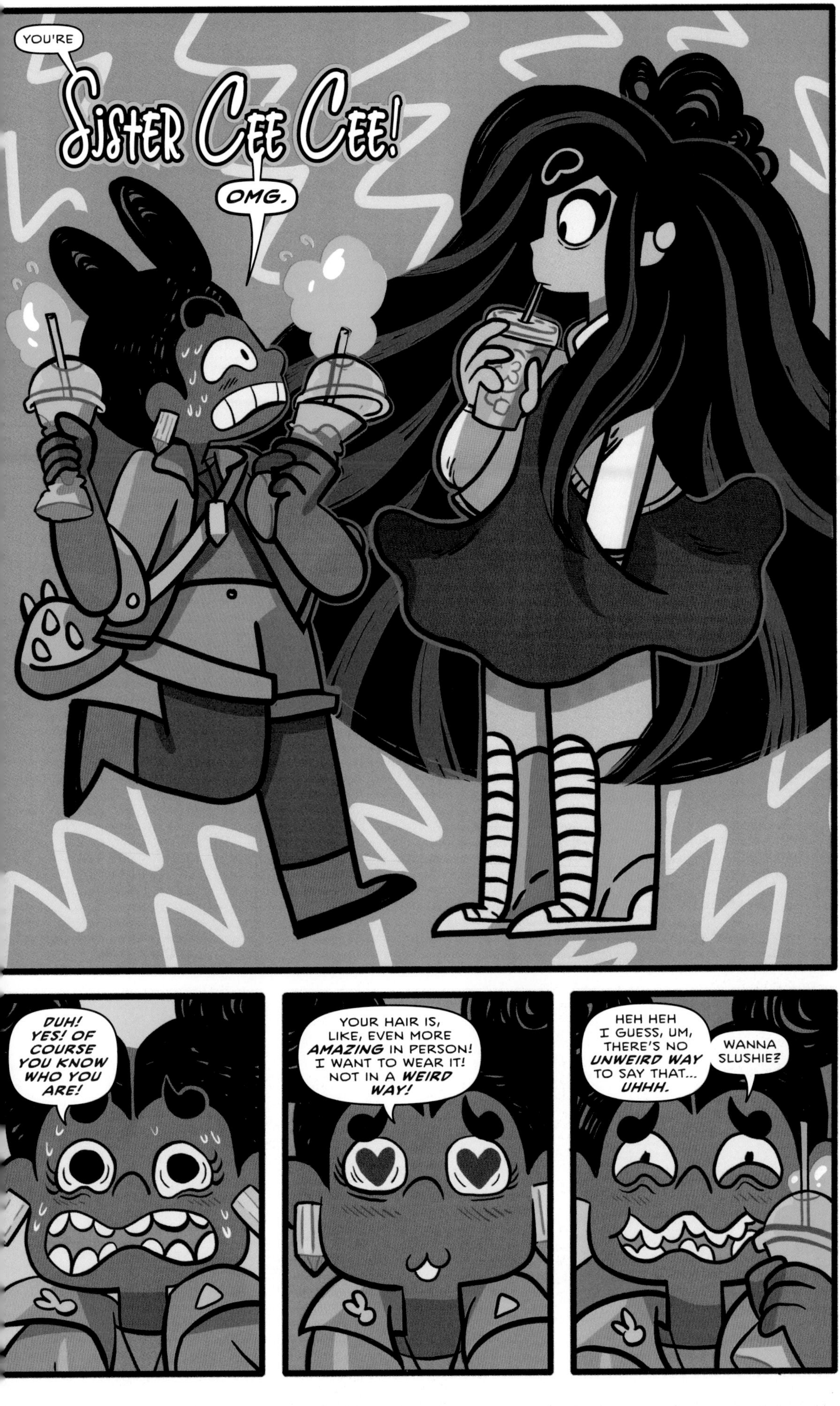
YOU'RE
SISTER CEE CEE!
OMG.
DUH! YES! OF COURSE YOU KNOW WHO YOU ARE!
YOUR HAIR IS, LIKE, EVEN MORE AMAZING IN PERSON! I WANT TO WEAR IT! NOT IN A WEIRD WAY!
HEH HEH I GUESS, UM, THERE'S NO UNWEIRD WAY TO SAY THAT... UHHH.
WANNA SLUSHIE?

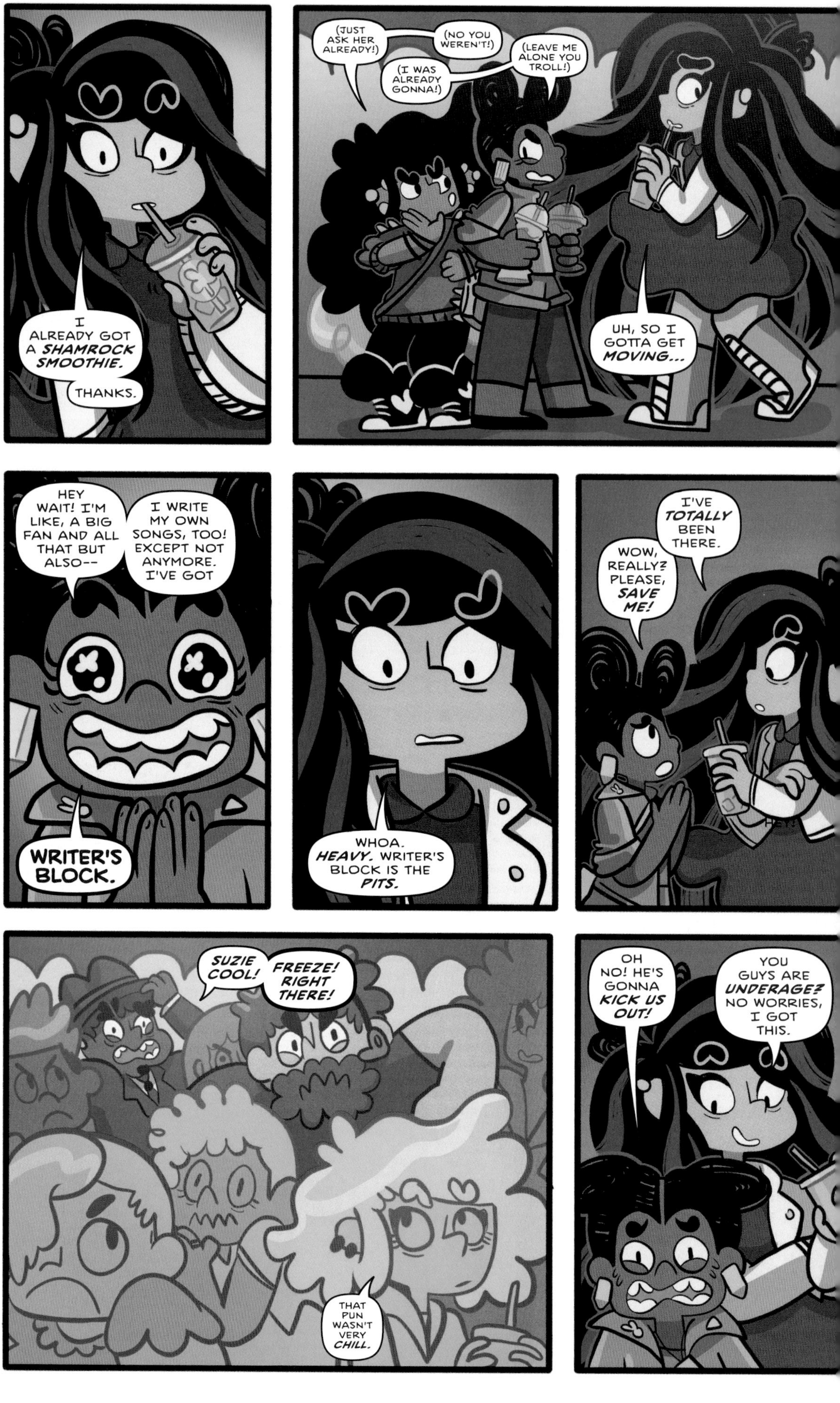
I ALREADY GOT A *SHAMROCK SMOOTHIE.*
THANKS.
(JUST ASK HER ALREADY!)
(I WAS ALREADY GONNA!)
(NO YOU WEREN'T!)
(LEAVE ME ALONE YOU TROLL!)
UH, SO I GOTTA GET *MOVING...*
HEY WAIT! I'M LIKE, A BIG FAN AND ALL THAT BUT ALSO--
I WRITE MY OWN SONGS, TOO! EXCEPT NOT ANYMORE. I'VE GOT
WRITER'S BLOCK.
WHOA. *HEAVY.* WRITER'S BLOCK IS THE *PITS.*
I'VE *TOTALLY* BEEN THERE.
WOW, REALLY? PLEASE, *SAVE ME!*
SUZIE COOL!
FREEZE! RIGHT THERE!
THAT PUN WASN'T VERY *CHILL.*
OH NO! HE'S GONNA *KICK US OUT!*
YOU GUYS ARE *UNDERAGE?* NO WORRIES, I GOT THIS.

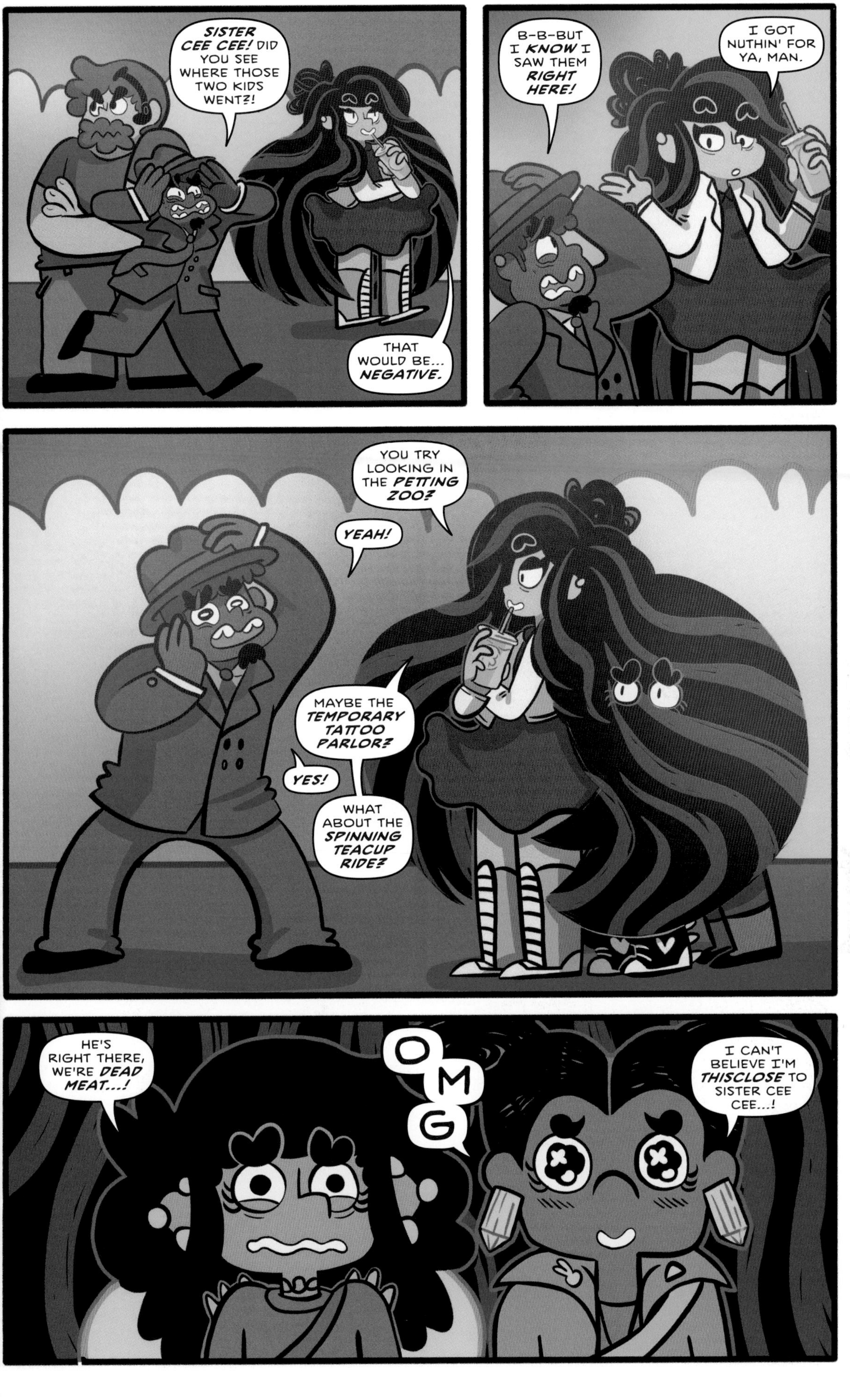
SISTER CEE CEE! DID YOU SEE WHERE THOSE TWO KIDS WENT?!
THAT WOULD BE... NEGATIVE.
B-B-BUT I KNOW I SAW THEM RIGHT HERE!
I GOT NUTHIN' FOR YA, MAN.
YOU TRY LOOKING IN THE PETTING ZOO?
YEAH!
MAYBE THE TEMPORARY TATTOO PARLOR?
YES!
WHAT ABOUT THE SPINNING TEACUP RIDE?
HE'S RIGHT THERE, WE'RE DEAD MEAT...!
OMG
I CAN'T BELIEVE I'M THISCLOSE TO SISTER CEE CEE...!

WHOA--
LOOK!

SHE
HAS A *NECK
TATTOO!*

SHE
BITES HER
NAILS, *LIKE
ME!*

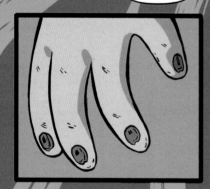

HER HAIR
SMELLS LIKE
A *CHRISTMAS
TREE!*

LOOK
AT HER *PRINCESS
CAT-THERINE*
CARDIGAN!

SHE
DOESN'T
*SHAVE HER
LEGS!*

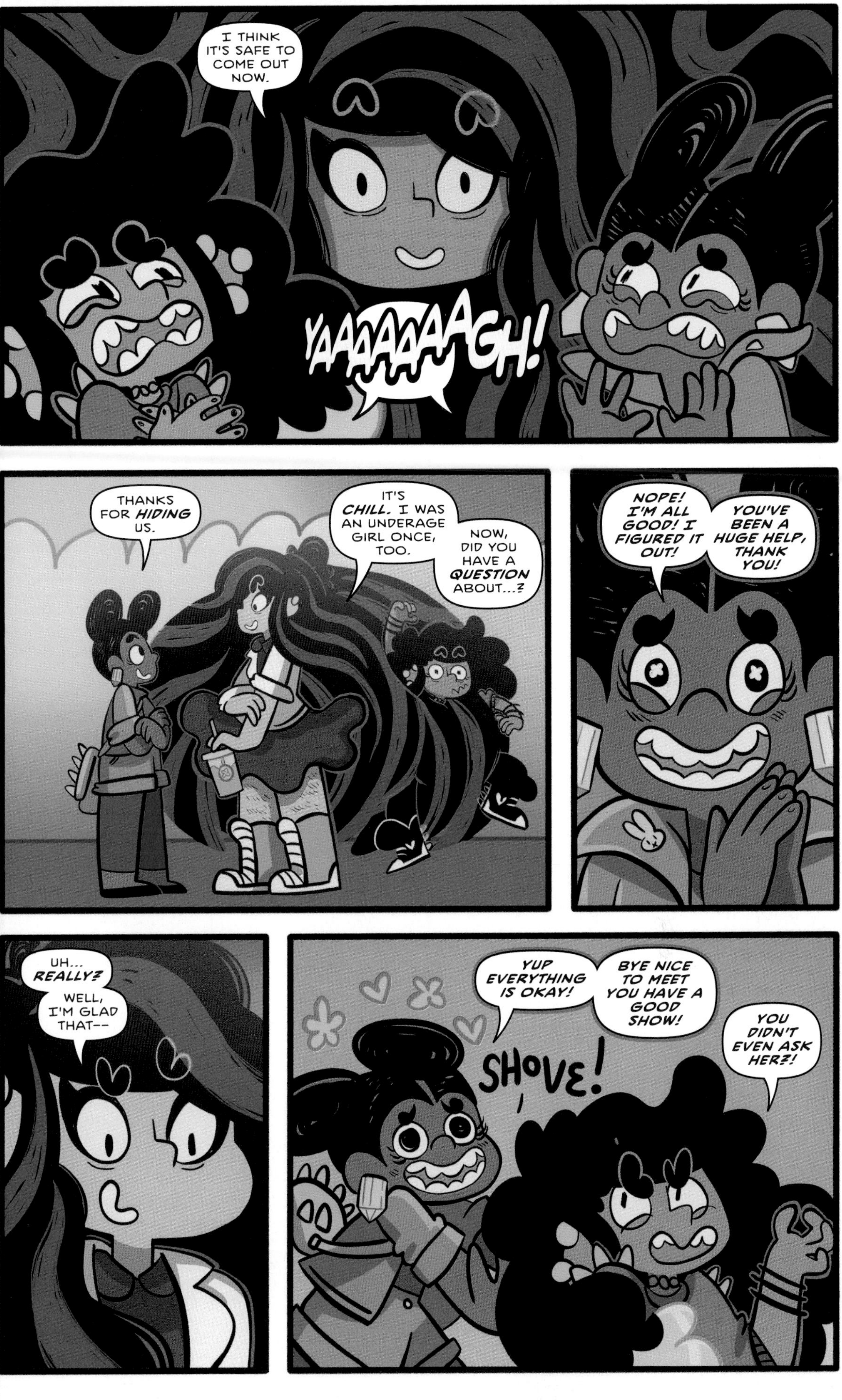
I THINK IT'S SAFE TO COME OUT NOW.
YAAAAAAAGH!
THANKS FOR *HIDING* US.
IT'S *CHILL.* I WAS AN UNDERAGE GIRL ONCE, TOO.
NOW, DID YOU HAVE A *QUESTION* ABOUT...?
NOPE! I'M ALL GOOD! I FIGURED IT OUT!
YOU'VE BEEN A HUGE HELP, THANK YOU!
UH... *REALLY?*
WELL, I'M GLAD THAT--
YUP EVERYTHING IS OKAY!
BYE NICE TO MEET YOU HAVE A GOOD SHOW!
SHOVE!
YOU DIDN'T EVEN ASK HER?!

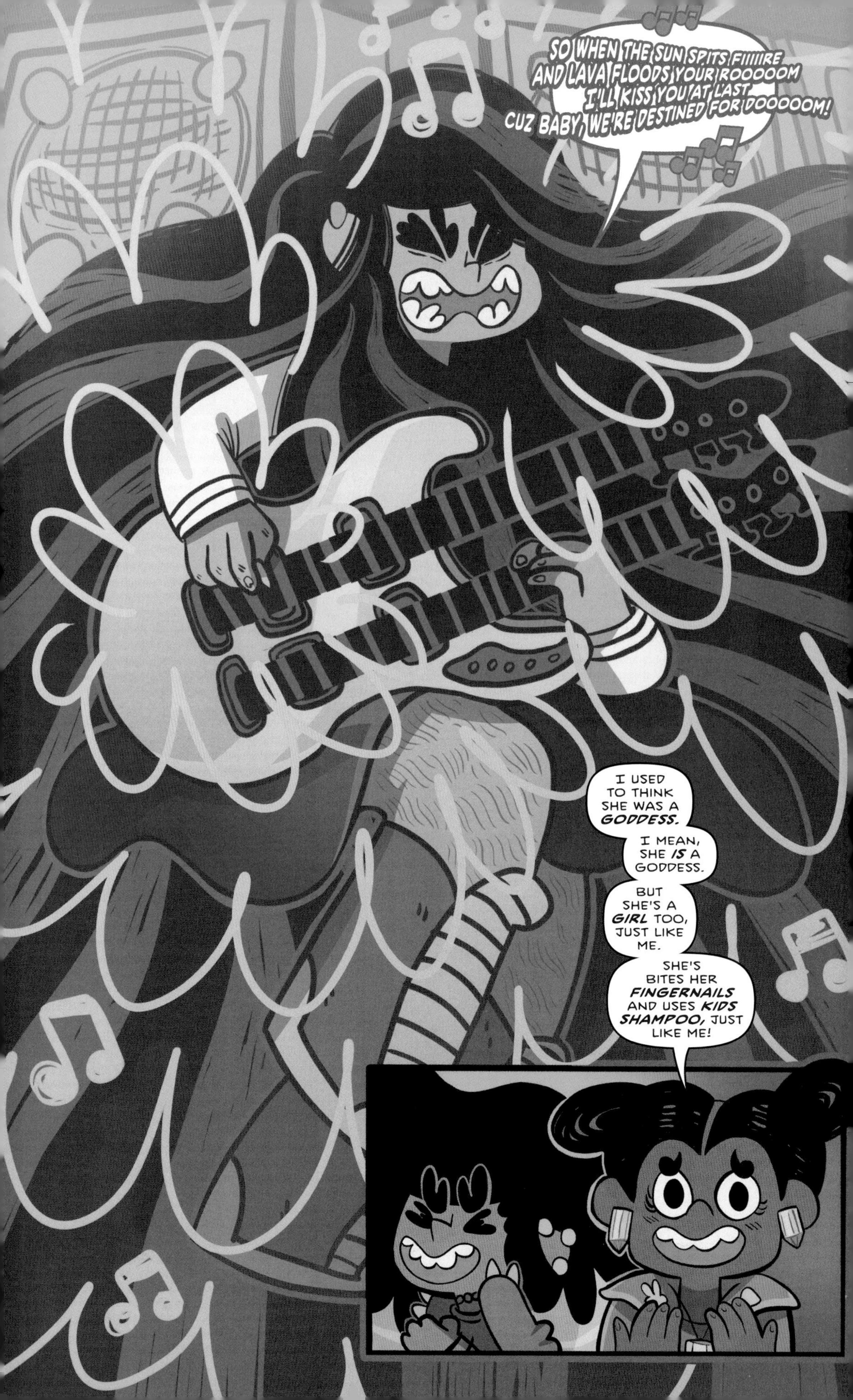
SO WHEN THE SUN SPITS FIIIIIRE AND LAVA FLOODS YOUR ROOOOOM I'LL KISS YOU AT LAST CUZ BABY, WE'RE DESTINED FOR DOOOOOM!
I USED TO THINK SHE WAS A GODDESS.
I MEAN, SHE IS A GODDESS.
BUT SHE'S A GIRL TOO, JUST LIKE ME.
SHE'S BITES HER FINGERNAILS AND USES KIDS SHAMPOO, JUST LIKE ME!

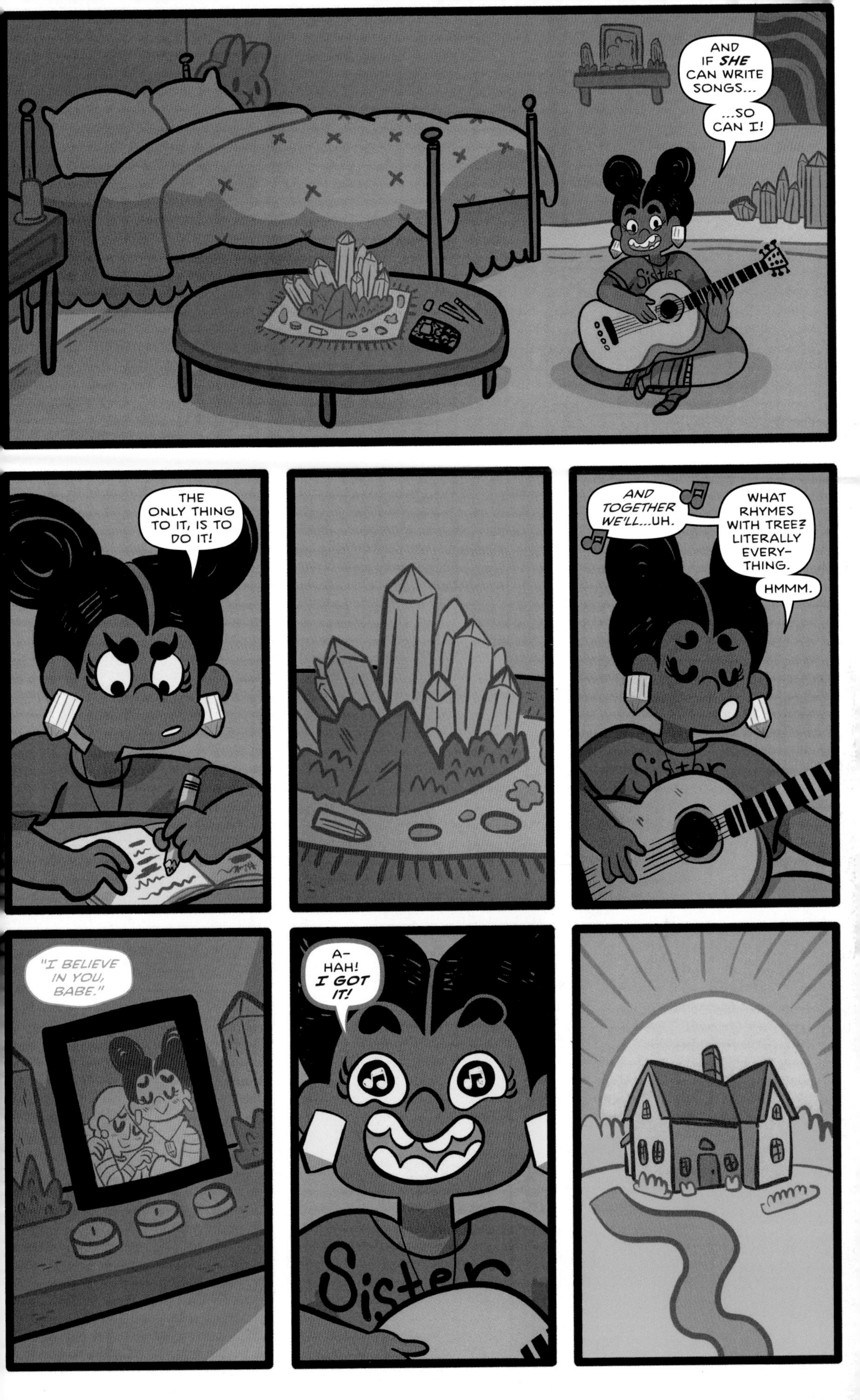
AND IF SHE CAN WRITE SONGS...
...SO CAN I!
THE ONLY THING TO IT, IS TO DO IT!
AND TOGETHER WE'LL...UH.
WHAT RHYMES WITH TREE? LITERALLY EVERY-THING.
HMMM.
"I BELIEVE IN YOU, BABE."
A-HAH! I GOT IT!

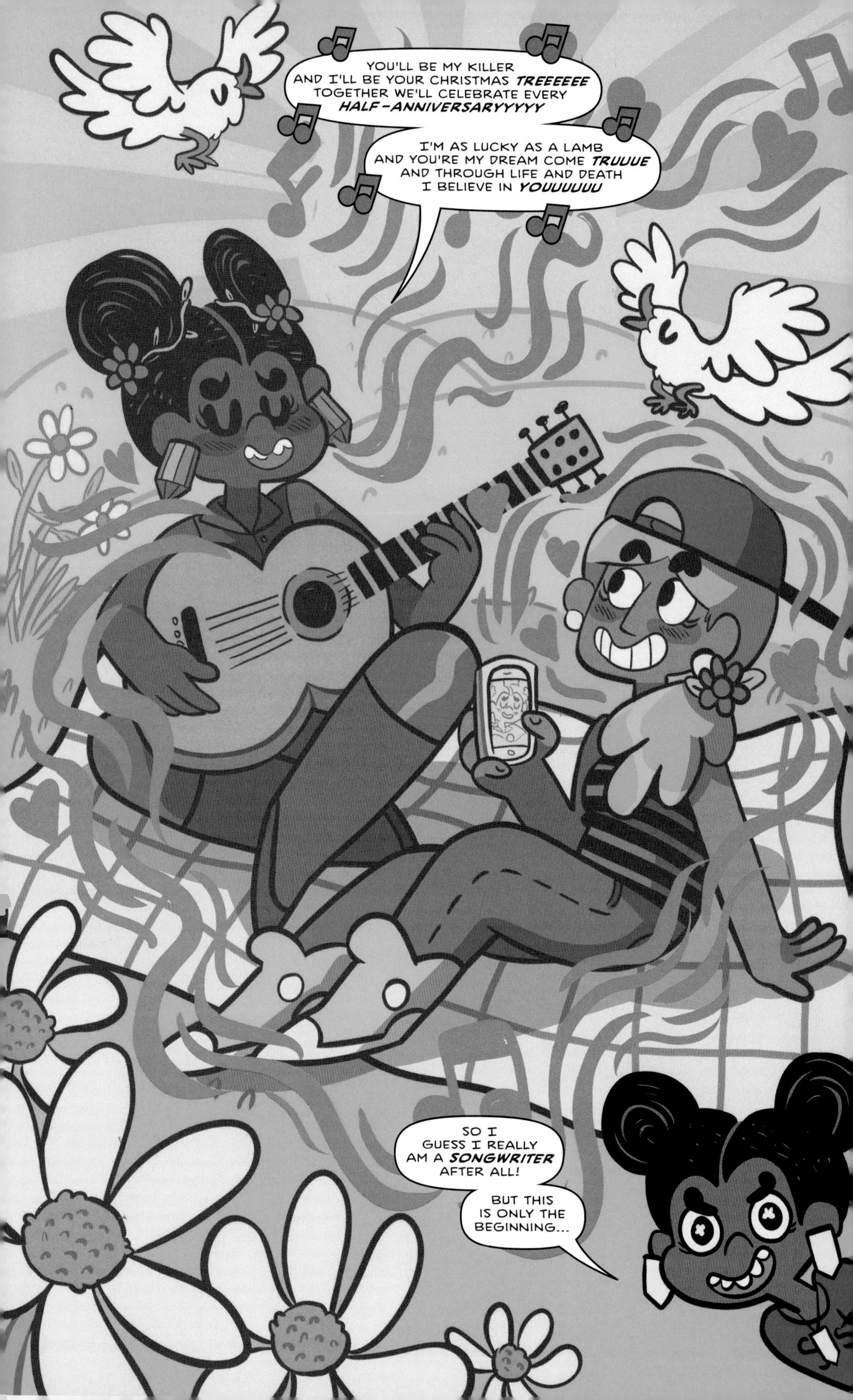

YOU'LL BE MY KILLER AND I'LL BE YOUR CHRISTMAS *TREEEEEE* TOGETHER WE'LL CELEBRATE EVERY *HALF-ANNIVERSARYYYYY*
I'M AS LUCKY AS A LAMB AND YOU'RE MY DREAM COME *TRUUUE* AND THROUGH LIFE AND DEATH I BELIEVE IN *YOUUUUUU*
SO I GUESS I REALLY AM A *SONGWRITER* AFTER ALL!
BUT THIS IS ONLY THE BEGINNING...

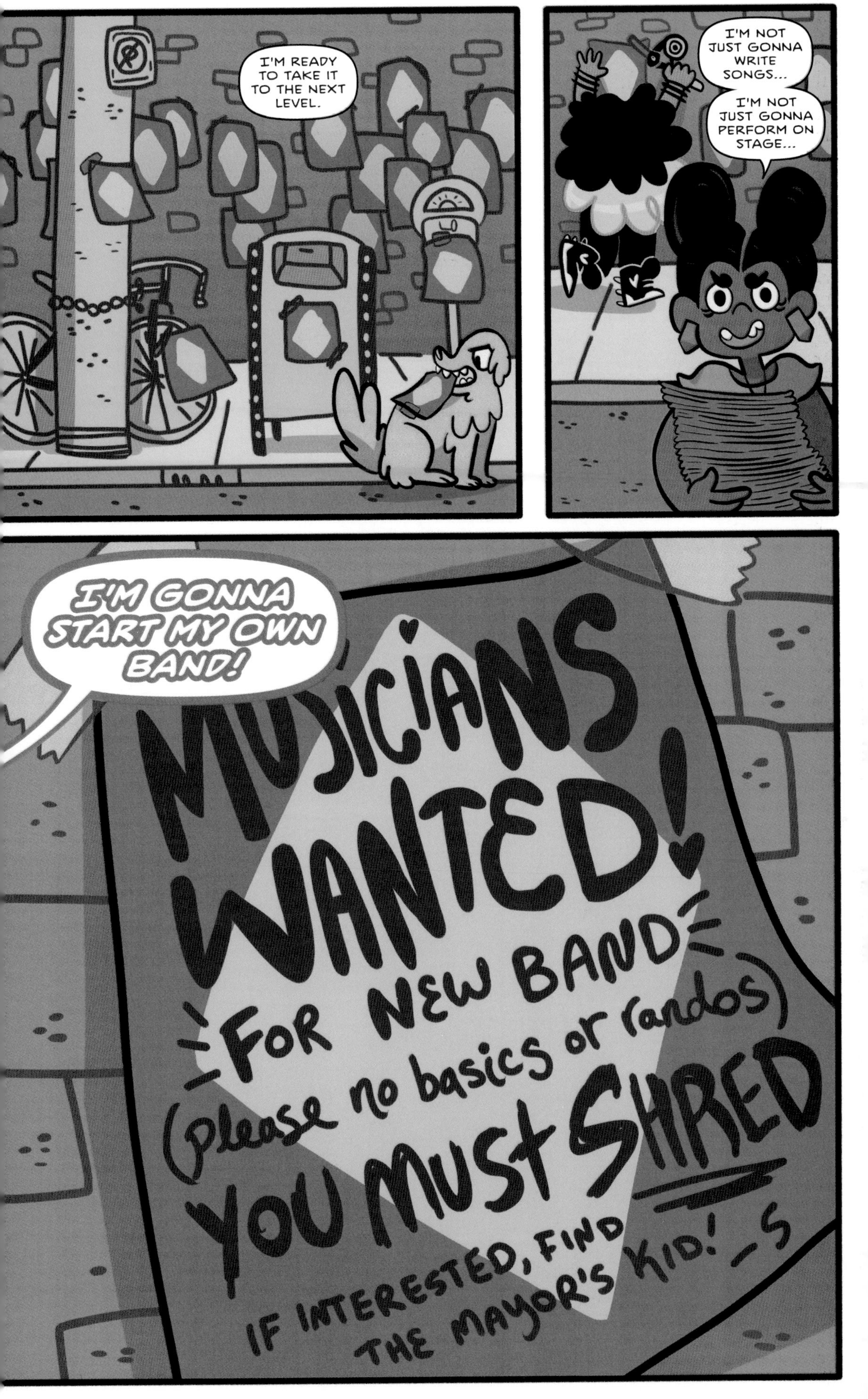
I'M READY TO TAKE IT TO THE NEXT LEVEL.
I'M NOT JUST GONNA WRITE SONGS...
I'M NOT JUST GONNA PERFORM ON STAGE...
I'M GONNA START MY OWN BAND!
MUSICIANS WANTED!
FOR NEW BAND
(please no basics or randos)
YOU MUST SHRED
IF INTERESTED, FIND THE MAYOR'S KID! _S

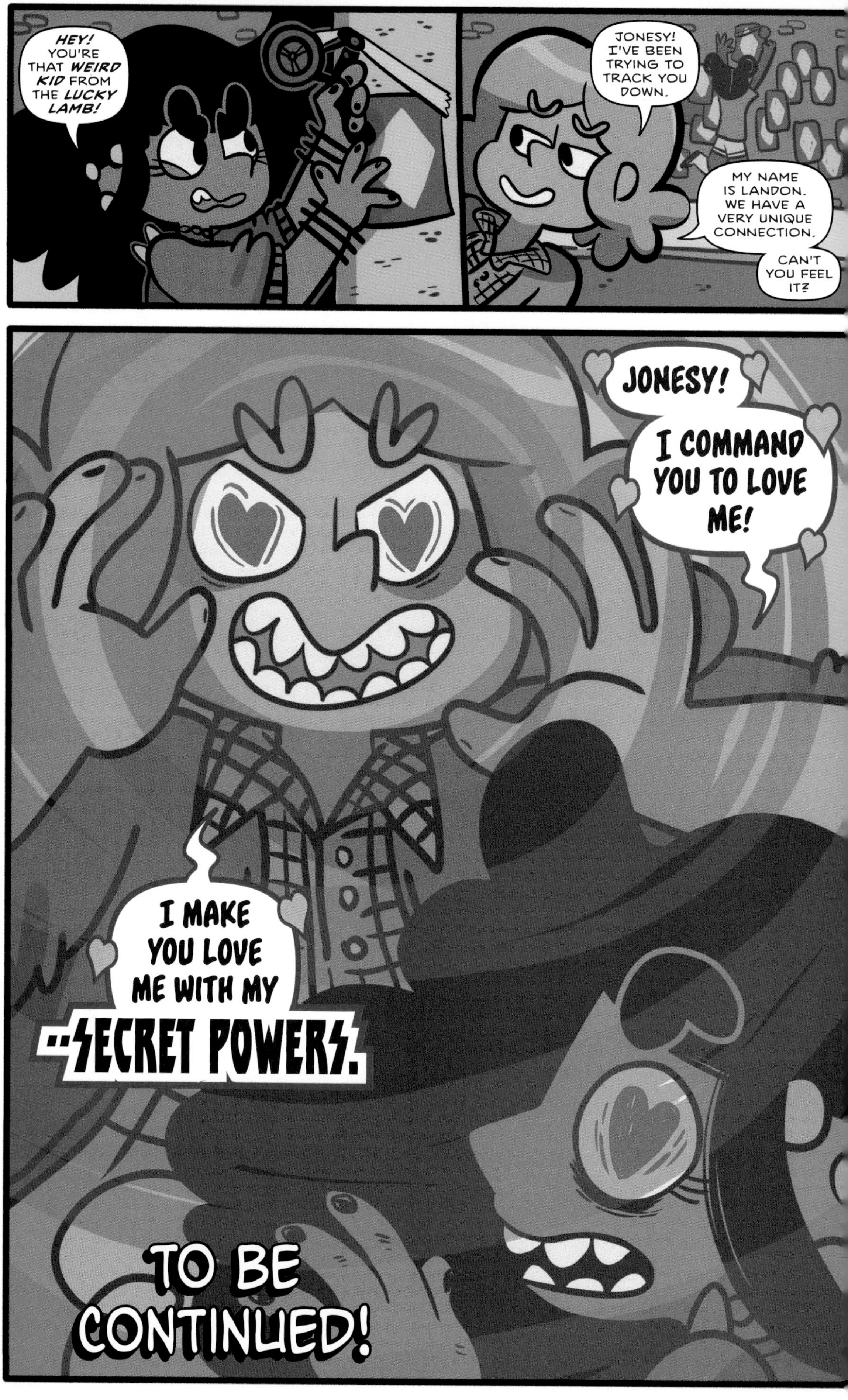
HEY! YOU'RE THAT WEIRD KID FROM THE LUCKY LAMB!
JONESY! I'VE BEEN TRYING TO TRACK YOU DOWN.
MY NAME IS LANDON. WE HAVE A VERY UNIQUE CONNECTION.
CAN'T YOU FEEL IT?
JONESY!
I COMMAND YOU TO LOVE ME!
I MAKE YOU LOVE ME WITH MY
...SECRET POWERS.
TO BE CONTINUED!

COVER GALLERY

ISSUE FIVE COVER BY
CAITLIN ROSE BOYLE
COLORS BY MICKEY QUINN

ISSUE FIVE SECOND PRINT COVER BY
NATACHA BUSTOS

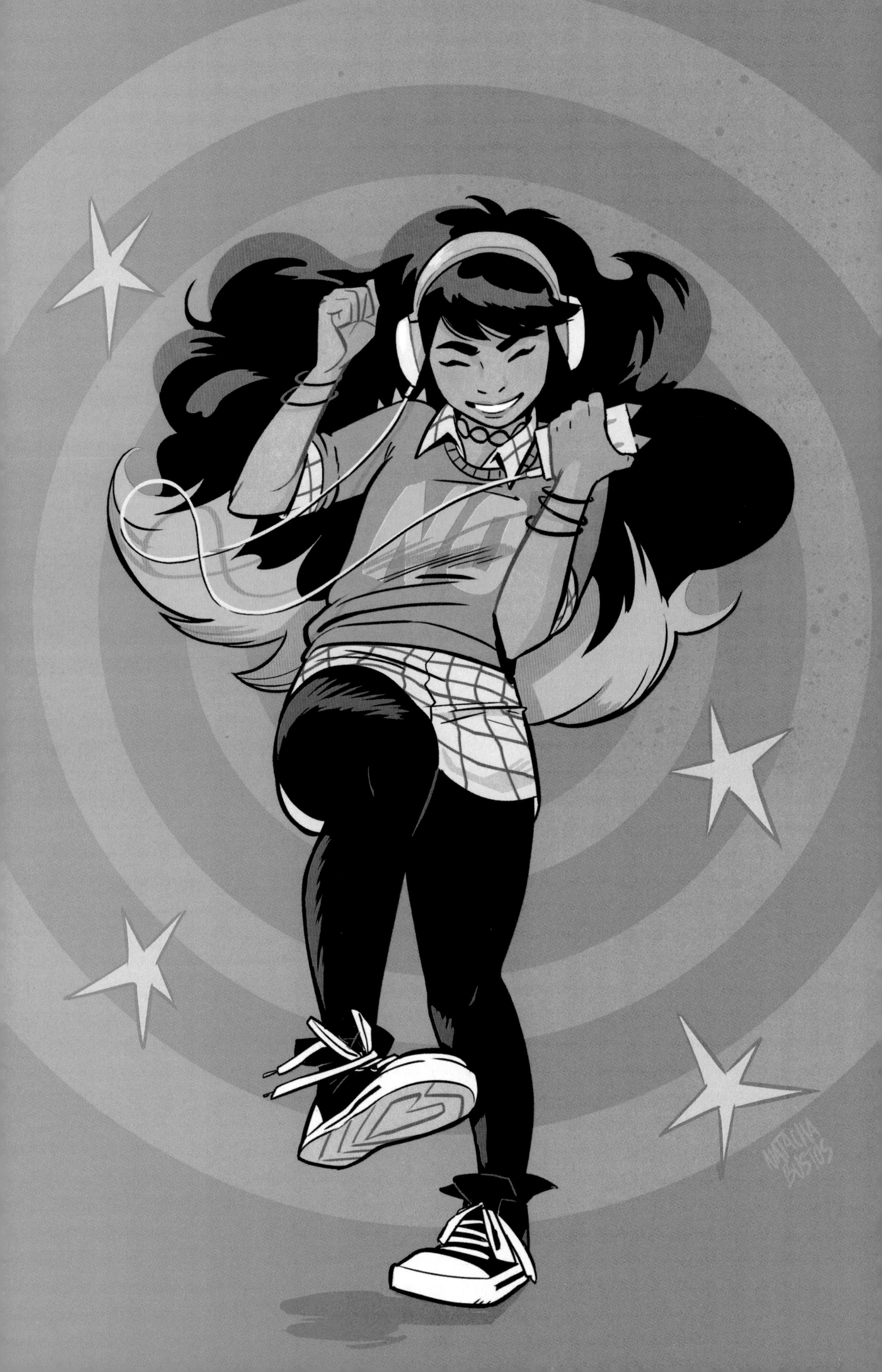
NATACHA BUSTOS

ISSUE SIX COVER BY
CAITLIN ROSE BOYLE
COLORS BY MICKEY QUINN

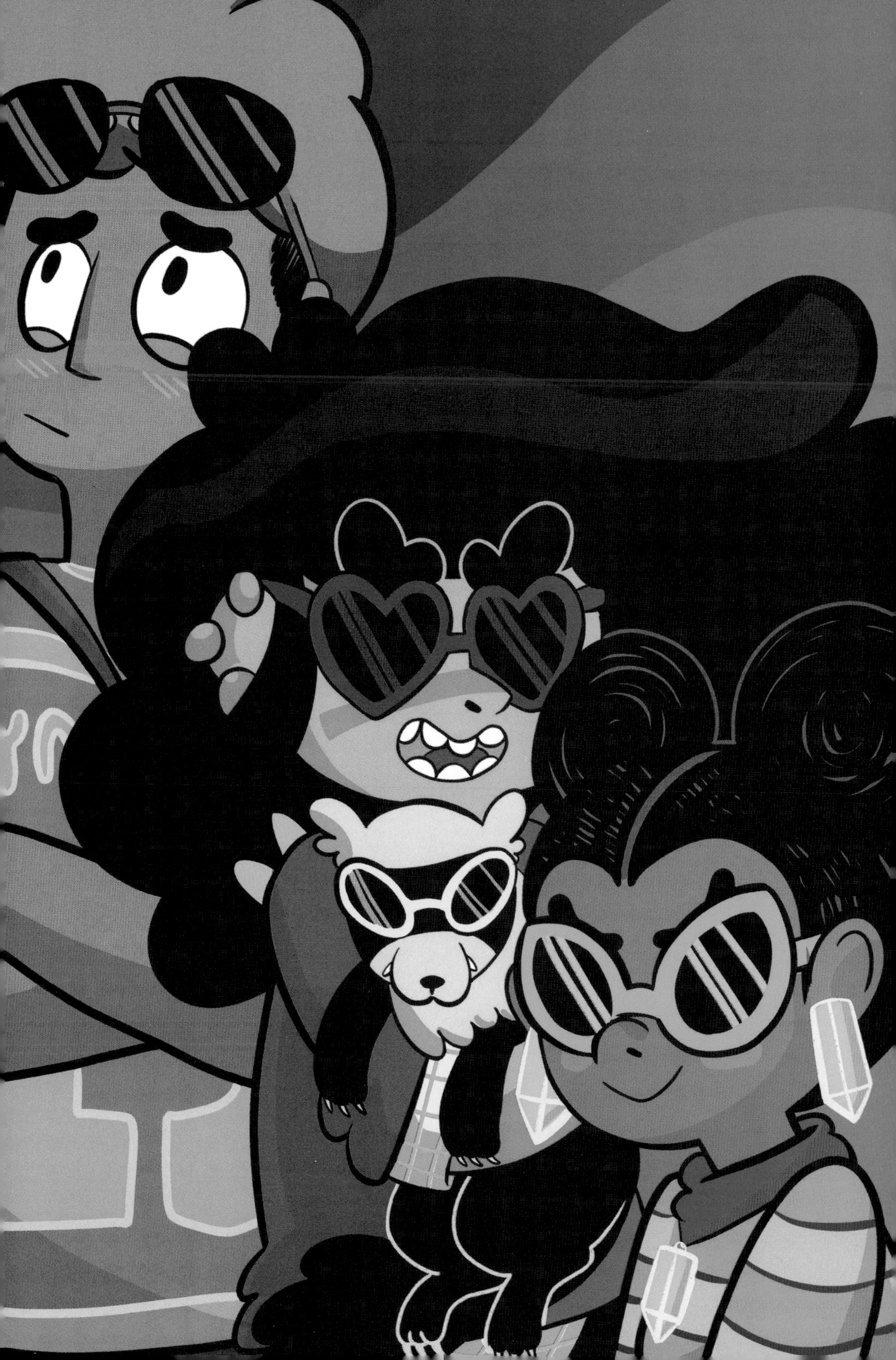

ISSUE SEVEN COVER BY
CAITLIN ROSE BOYLE
COLORS BY FRED C. STRESING

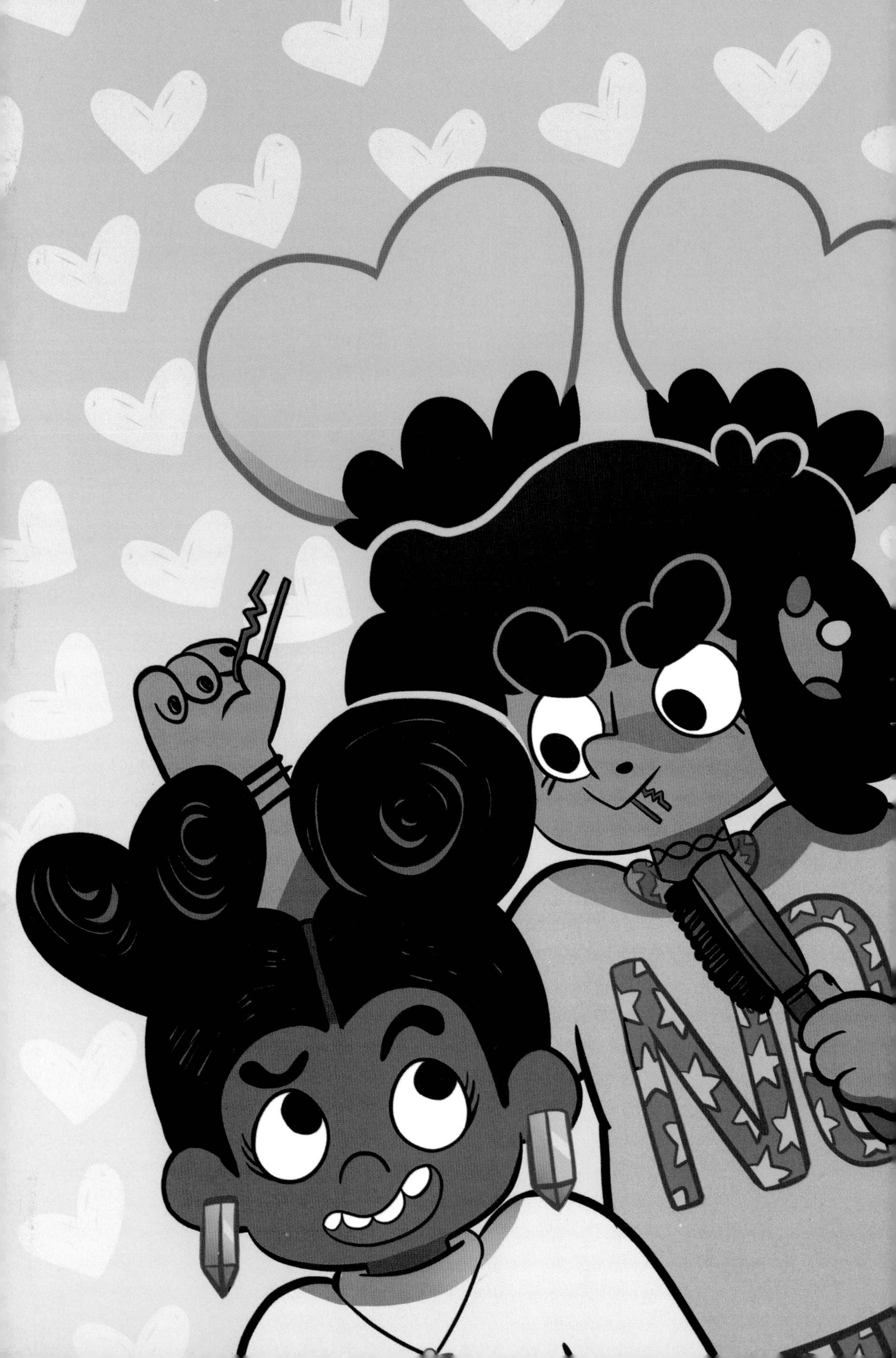

ISSUE EIGHT COVER BY
CAITLIN ROSE BOYLE
COLORS BY FRED C. STRESING

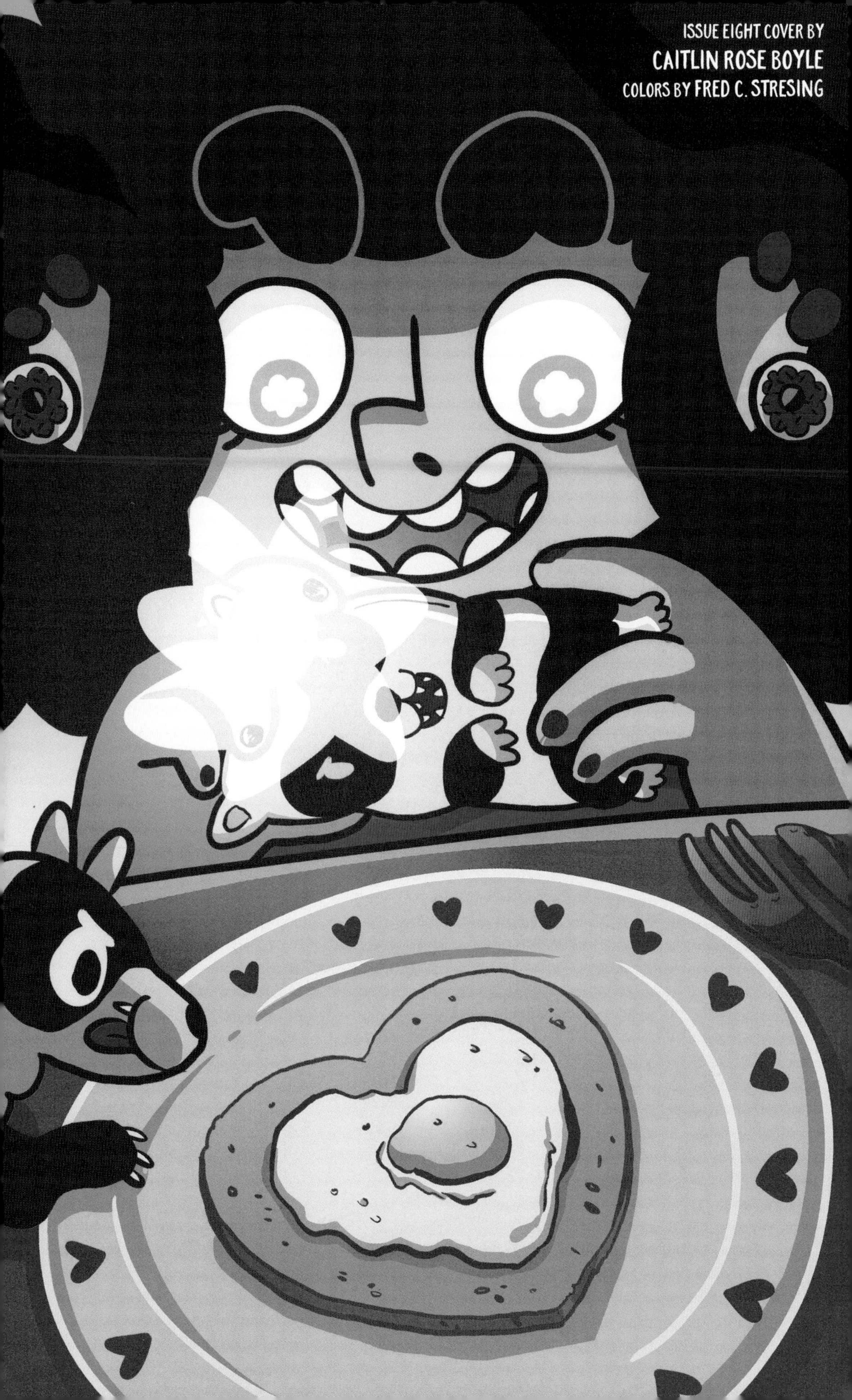

DEVELOPMENT SKETCHES AND COMMENTARY BY
CAITLIN ROSE BOYLE

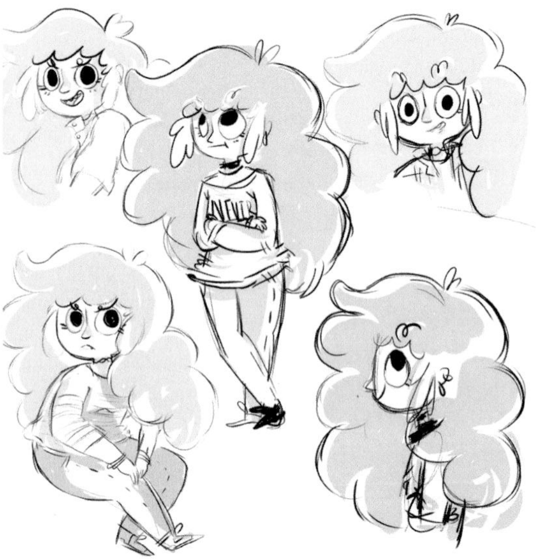

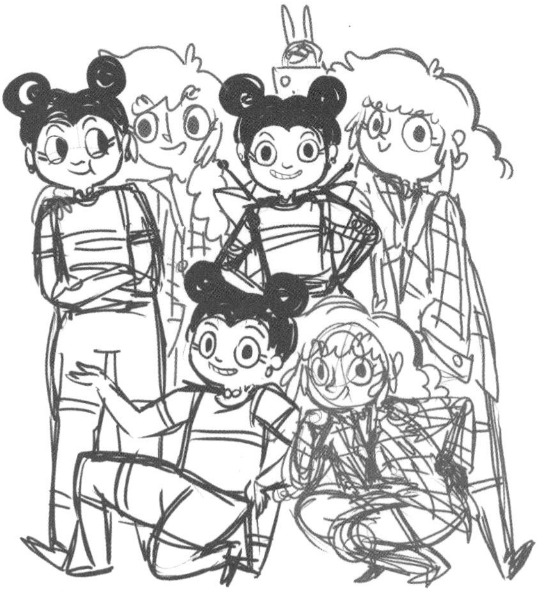

1 I wanted to do a series of sketches of Jonesy just emoting and being a person – she's a little softer here than she is in the comics. The eyebrows and hair are still wrong, but her face is starting to come together.

2 Susan is starting to come together here – Susan is way shorter than Jonesy in a lot of the concept art! I had't figured out her height or her style yet – early Susan looks like she raided Jonesy's closet.

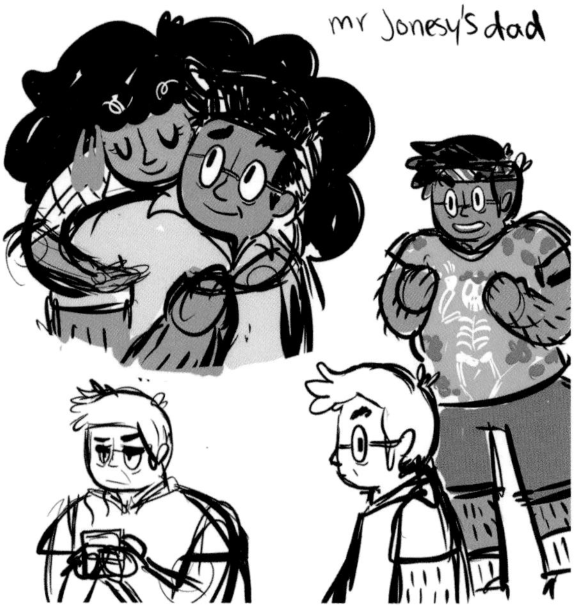
mr Jonesy's dad

3 Really early Dad concept art! I didn't finalize his look until I started drawing issue 1.

Friend?

4 I think this is the first drawing where she's sporting shoulder studs? I like to think she bulk ordered a bag of studs online and is just slowly studding her entire wardrobe. Can you stud socks??? Jonesy will find out.

5 These are the first Susan sketches, back before she even had a name - I remember distinctly that Sam's note was BIGGER HAIR BUNS. Which was a really really good note that I continue to run with.

6 This is an early Jonesy & Susan drawing that eventually became the cover to issue 2! Susan's style is still weird, but her hair is on point.

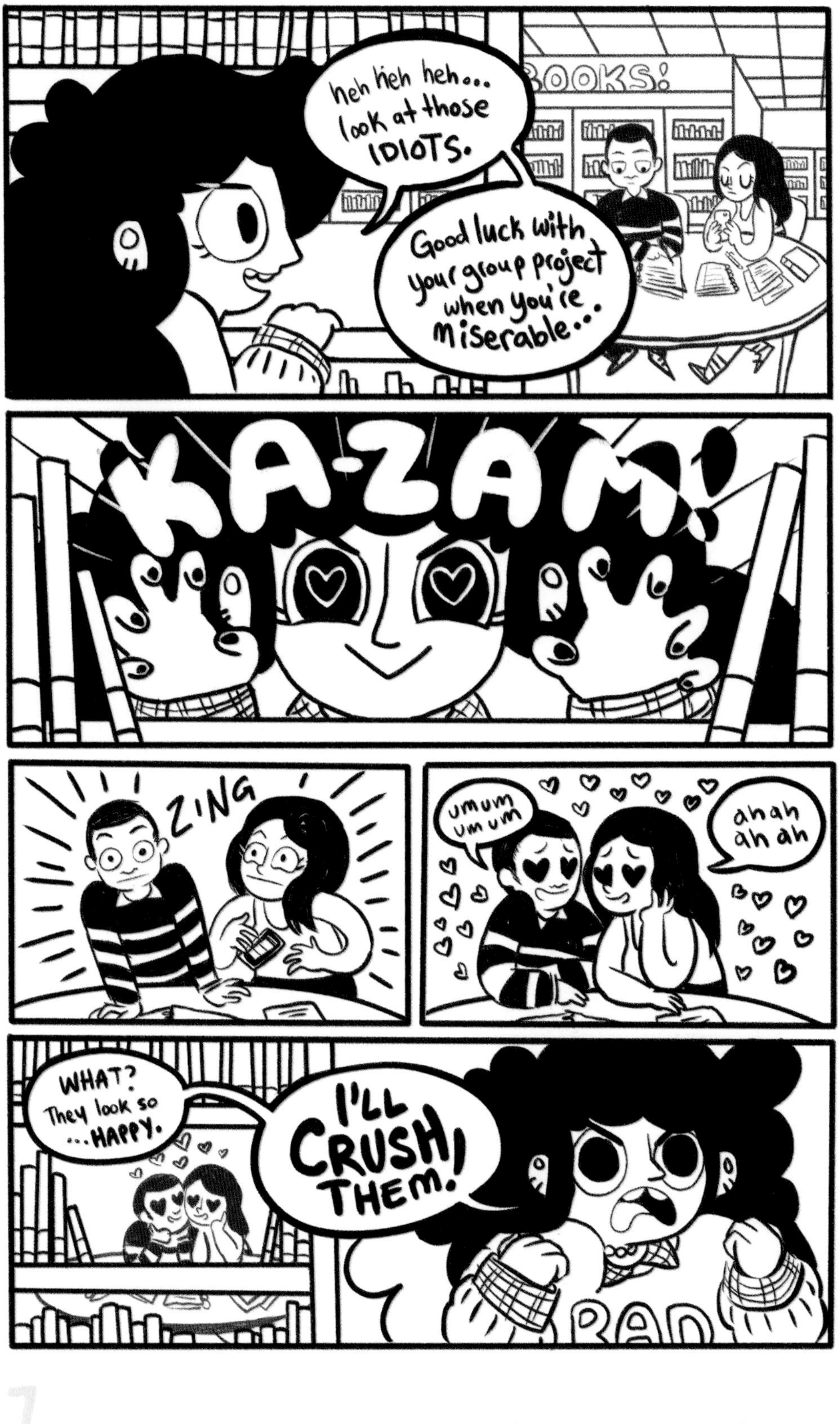
heh heh heh... look at those IDIOTS.
Good luck with your group project when you're miserable...
BOOKS!
KA-ZAM!
ZING
umum umum
ahah ahah
WHAT? They look so ...HAPPY.
I'LL CRUSH THEM!
RAD

7

This is the comic we put together to pitch BOOM! It's pretty close to the final style I landed on for issue one – here you get to see what *JONESY* would have looked like if I hand lettered the entire thing. Shudder...

CREATOR BIOS

SAM HUMPHRIES is a comic book writer. He broke into comics with the self-published runaway hits *Our Love Is Real* and *Sacrifice*. Since then, he has written high profile books such as *Legendary Star-Lord* for Marvel, *Green Lanterns* for DC Comics, and *Citizen Jack* for Image Comics. He lives in Los Angeles with his girlfriend and their cats, El Niño and Hopey.

CAITLIN ROSE BOYLE is a cartoonist who spends way too much time on the internet. Like way, way, way too much time. She co-created the Short Toon *Buck N' Lou & The Night Crew* for Nickelodeon's 2014 Shorts Program. Jonesy is her first comic book series, and now the longest running project she's ever worked on! Caitlin currently resides in Pittsburgh with her partner and a window full of houseplants.

BRITTANY PEER is a Colorist who spends most of her free time laying on the floor of her office with her cat. She has worked on IDW's *TMNT Casey & April*, quite a few indie projects, and has been featured in various anthologies.

COREY BREEN has been a professional in the comic book industry for over fifteen years, thirteen of which were for DC Entertainment. As a Sr. Pre-Press Artist, he has contributed art, lettering, color and more to thousands of comic books and other media. Having left DC Entertainment in 2013 to move down to Virginia, Corey is now a superhero in his own right. He is a head designer at a top investment firm company by day, and continues to work in the comic book industry as a freelancer by night. He currently enjoys lettering some of DC and BOOM! Studios' fan favorite books. Corey lives with his loving wife, Kristy, toddler son Tyler, and three cats.

MATTHEW LEVINE is an assistant editor at BOOM! Studios who appreciates the art of a well made deli sandwich. He's worked in television as a writer's assistant and has self published his own comic. He lives in Los Angeles, where he's also from.

JEANINE SCHAEFER has been editing comics for over ten years. She's worked at both Marvel and DC, and her current titles include the upcoming *Motor Crush* and *Prima* from Image Comics. She founded *Girl Comics*, an anthology celebrating the history of women at Marvel, and edited the Eisner-nominated Marvel YA title, *Mystic*. She lives in Los Angeles with her husband and two kids, and sporadically runs a tumblr celebrating the special relationship between nerds and cats.

SHANNON WATTERS is an editor at BOOM! Studios and the head of its BOOM! Box and KaBOOM! imprints. She is also the co-creator and co-writer of the Eisner Award-winning comic book series *Lumberjanes*. She lives in Los Angeles with her beautiful Canadian wife and their exceptionally adorable dog.